TO CHA ⌐⌐LANDER

THE SUTHERLANDS OF DORNOCH CASTLE ~ BOOK 5

CALLIE HUTTON

Copyright © 2023 by Callie Hutton

All rights reserved.

No part of this book may be reproduced in any form or by any electronic or mechanical means, including information storage and retrieval systems, without written permission from the author, except for the use of brief quotations in a book review.

This book is 100% created by the author. No AI was used.

ABOUT THE BOOK

Love blossoms amidst secrets and suspicion...

Lady Donella Sutherland has been ignored by most of her clan because she is thought to be simple-minded. She wasn't always that way, her brother, Laird Haydon insists. But the years go on and she doesn't change.

Callum Gunn, second oldest son to Laird Gunn has been accused by his brother, Fraser of causing his father's death on the battlefield. A charge Callum strongly denies. With a few men willing to testify on Laird Fraser Gunn's behalf, Callum finds himself banned from his clan.

A few months of wandering around brings him to the Sutherland Castle where he asks Laird Haydon Sutherland to allow him to join his warrior forces. Not trustful of the Gunn Clan, Haydon refuses, but as Callum is about to leave, Lady Donella slips on the stairs and after smacking her head on a stone step, tumbles down, right into Callum's arms.

Grateful for saving his sister from a certain death, Haydon allows Callum to stay.

When Donella awakens, she is surprised to find everyone treating her like a bairn. Her family and the clansfolk all act strangely toward her as she moves around the castle, doing normal jobs.

Callum finds the lass he rescued beautiful and charming. He sees nothing dimwitted about Donella and is confused by what he hears from others in the clan. However, as they grow closer he believes she is hiding a secret that could keep them from having a life together. If he wants that life with Donella, he must uncover what secrets she's been hiding.

* * *

Receive a free book and stay up to date with new releases and sales!
http://calliehutton.com/newsletter/

1

Dornoch Castle
Home of the Sutherland Clan
July, 1660

Lady Donella Sutherland, sister to Laird Haydon Sutherland and Conall Sutherland, had seen three and twenty summers and yet remained unmarried. She was sure her laird, like everyone else in the clan, thought her simple-minded, and therefore he had ne'er tried to arrange a marriage for her.

Donella was no' simple-minded. Her mind was locked down by fear and guilt. Thwarted by memories she'd kept to herself.

And had been since she was a lass. No one kenned that because she ne'er told anyone what had happened to her and what she'd done when she was a mere fourteen years.

That was when she drew into herself and blocked out the rest of the world. It was the only way she could protect herself. She had her own secret safe place in her head where she lived most of the time. She spent hours in the woods enclosed within the castle walls, walking, and enjoying the sights and sounds. Avoiding people was her favorite thing to do.

In the wintertime, she took hour long walks in the snow, loving the cool air on her face. It was never too cold for her because she was free.

"Donella, there ye are, lass." Her sister-by-marriage, Ainslee, Haydon's wife, called out to her where she sat against a tree, drawing on the parchment paper Haydon was able to get for her. She knew it was an expense, but since she asked for nothing more, he'd oftentimes told her she deserved it.

She wasn't sure what she deserved, if anything. But did not like to dwell on it since being in her happy place where difficult thoughts didn't exist was much more pleasant.

Ainslee approached, her stride forceful, her long braid bouncing over her shoulder. Donella wondered where the woman got all her energy. She ran the keep like a warrior and even kept her four bairns and one—difficult at times—husband in line. Haydon thought he ran the clan, but Ainslee had more to do with it than he did, although no one would e'er say that to his face. However, with as crazy in love as he was with his wife, he would most likely laugh and walk away.

Her sister-by-marriage came to an abrupt halt in front of her. "I need yer help in the kitchen."

"Aye." Donella gathered up her things and stood. She brushed off the back of her dress and smiled at Ainslee. "What do ye need me for?"

Ainslee patted her on the shoulder, a slight shiver running down Donelle's arm at the touch. "Since ye took over the garden again, I must tell ye Jonet is so verra happy to have fresh herbs to season the meals with. Ye do have a gift."

Donella's eyes grew wide. It was rare for anyone to notice something she did and offer a compliment about it. After Mam died and Donella's world fell apart, she let everything in the castle go, even though she was supposed to be acting as chatelaine. Back then, she couldn't even look at the garden without turning into a waterpot. That was where she and Mam spent so many hours, talking, and making Donella feel safe and loved.

"Thank ye, Ainslee. I do enjoy working out there. Is something amiss?"

Ainslee turned and they both began to walk toward the keep. "A bit. Muriel, the young maid Jonet sent out to gather herbs for the meal she is preparing, apparently dinna ken one plant from another and brought back all the wrong things. Jonet wants ye to gather what she needs because 'tis growing late, and also, if ye will, dry and preserve the herbs Muriel brought in so as not to go to waste."

Having something to do using her hands, keeping her mind occupied was fine with her. She gladly tucked her drawings away and followed Ainslee to the kitchen back door.

"Donella, lass, here's a basket for ye to gather the herbs I need." Jonet, the cook who'd been with them for years smiled as she handed it to her. The friendly woman was the solution to another mistake Donella had made. Shortly after she'd taken over the chatelaine's duties following Mam's death, Donella had hired the prior cook, Margie, who had turned out to be a verra poor choice.

The cook had terrorized the kitchen staff, had been rude to the laird and his wife, and after Haydon fired her, they discovered she'd been stealing from them. Nothing Donella seemed to do to manage the keep had been the right thing.

Donnella gladly took the basket. This was a task she thoroughly enjoyed. The smells of the garden and the earthly aroma of all the wonderful herbs that Jonet used in her dishes surrounded her, bringing her peace.

She was happy Ainslee had put her in charge of the garden when she'd married Hayden. By then she'd gotten over the hardest part of losing Mam. Now only good memories enveloped her when she knelt on the soft, damp ground and completed her chore.

* * *

CALLUM GUNN KICKED a clod of dirt and stamped out the small fire he'd used to cook the plump pigeon he'd caught for his meal. Certain that all was well, he then packed up his few possessions and tightened the cord holding them to Favela's haunches. The poor animal was looking as scrawny as Callum.

It was time to approach one of the clans who could use his warrior skills. After wandering for weeks, he realized the closest clan was Sutherland. Callum threw his leg over his horse's back and moved them in the direction of Dornoch Castle. He went over in his mind what he kenned of the clan.

A verra old clan and an honorable one, Laird Haydon Sutherland had a brother and cousin who held the positions of seconds-in-command. He wasn't looking for a position like that. He only wanted to feel part of a group.

With war forever a threat, a clan could always use another sword. His had always been the finest, the best of the Gunn's. 'Twas tired he was of wandering; he wanted a place to rest his head with a roof over it and regular hot meals. He also craved a sense of being needed.

He rode for a few hours, the sun just beginning to set when he approached the castle.

"Who goes there and what is your business?" The warrior on the Dornoch Castle rampart called down to him as Callum grew closer to the drawbridge.

"I am Callum Gunn and I wish to speak with Laird Sutherland."

The man studied him for a minute, looking around the area as if expecting hordes of warriors to emerge from the woods. The guard seemed to want to decide whether to throw hot oil on him or let him see the laird. "Come inside and drop your sword, and I will have someone meet you."

The drawbridge eased down, the squeals of the chain ringing in the evening air. Callum rode on, Fauvel's hooves clattering over the wood. He approached the portcullis, which raised, allowing him into the outer bailey.

The portcullis closed behind him, and several warriors stood in a small semi-circle behind one mon, a different warrior than the one on the rampart. His hand firmly rested on his sword as he approached him, then his massive warrior's body came to a full stop a few steps away and he drew out his sword. "Drop your sword and any knives or other weapons you have on ye."

Callum pulled his sword from the scabbard on his back. He also removed the sword by his side, and the knives strapped to his thigh, chest, and belt. When he was through, he stepped away from the pile. 'Twas a good thing the Sutherlands were known to be men of honor or there was no doubt he would be a dead mon.

The warrior collected the weapons. "Stay here and I will see if the laird wishes to speak with you." He turned and left, taking the armor with him, making Callum happy that he hadn't found the knife strapped to the back of his belt, under his leine and deer skin jerkin.

The other men continued to stand, their hands resting on the swords by their side. He waited more than a quarter of an hour before another man approached him. With no warmth in his greeting, he said, "I am Conall Sutherland, brother to the Laird of Sutherland." He crossed his arms over his chest. "What brings you to us today?"

"I would prefer to speak directly to the laird."

"It doona matter to me what ye prefer. The mon who let ye in said ye were Callum Gunn. Do ye come today representing yer laird?

"Nay."

Silence surrounded them as Conall glared at him. "Are ye aware that the Sutherlands are not on the best of terms with yer clan?"

"The Gunns are not my clan."

Sutherland stared at him for a moment. "What is your relationship to Laird Gunn?"

Callum spat on the ground. "He is my brother."

Conall raised his eyebrows. "I ken yer da died in a battle a couple of months ago. Why are ye here? Did yer brother toss ye out?"

"I left." Callum spread his feet apart. "We had a difference of opinions."

"Serious enough to make ye leave yer clan?"

"Aye."

Silence reigned for at least a full minute. Callum was growing weary of the mon's attitude. It wasna in his best interest to antagonize him, though. With as much control as he could muster, he said, "Am I going to see the laird?"

Conall shook his head. "Nay. The mon is busy. If ye have a message, ye can tell me and I'll pass the word onto him." He nodded at the front door and turned toward the steps he'd come down. "Ye can pick up your weapons when ye leave the outer bailey."

It dinna go as well as he'd hoped. He kenned it would be difficult to join another clan, especially one as powerful as the Sutherlands and who were not in the best of graces with the Gunns. He had hoped, however, to at least be able to speak with the laird.

Frustrated, he turned and with the men who had been watching the exchange following behind him, he started toward the door when he heard a loud scream. He looked over toward the stone staircase on the other side of the room where a young lass was frantically waving her arms as she slipped and began to tumble down.

Being the closest to her, he raced in her direction. She smacked her head against one of the stones in the wall but landed in his outstretched arms with a thump, almost tossing them both to the ground. Her eyes slowly closed.

A red stain grew on his leine where blood dripped from her head. The lass was out cold. He turned with her in his arms and yelled, "We need a healer here."

2

The lass in his arms, Callum hurried up the stairs after one of the warriors to the first floor. A large mon thundered down the corridor, almost shaking the several hundred-year-old stone floor and wall loose. The size and presence of the mon had to be Laird Haydon Sutherland. "Christ's toes, what the hell is going on? Who screamed?"

After glancing at Callum and the lass in his arms, he shouted, "Ainslee!" His roar bounced off the walls.

"I'm here, Haydon, no need to scare the animals in the stables with yer bellowing. I just heard a scream and came as fast as I could."

"'Twould be helpful if someone can tell me where to lay the lass down and then send for a healer," Callum shouted.

Haydon's eyes narrowed. "Who the hell are ye and why are ye holding the bleeding lass?"

Ainslee, who must have been the laird's wife, waved at her husband. "Stop, husband. Ye can see the lass is injured." She turned to Callum with a slight lift of her chin. "Ye can bring her in here." She turned and led the way.

Callum followed Lady Sutherland into a bedchamber a few doors down from where they stood. The laird followed them inside. Lady Sutherland whipped the bedcovers off in a flash. "Lay her down here."

Once Callum had easily placed her on the bed, another woman carrying a basket came bustling into the room. "What happened to Donella?"

Three pairs of eyes fixed on him. The laird with a great deal of suspicion, Lady Sutherland with concern for the lass and the other woman with raised brows, obviously waiting for someone to tell them what had happened.

Callum cleared his throat. "I was leaving the keep—" he looked at the laird—"as I was ordered to do, and I heard a scream. The lass had slipped on the stone steps. She grabbed for the wall, but was unsuccessful and tumbled down, smacking her head on one of the stones. I was able to catch her before she landed on the floor to keep her from worse injures."

The laird ran his hand down his face. "Are ye the Gunn Conall told to leave?"

He nodded. "Aye."

"Wait for me downstairs in the great hall. Have one of the lasses bring ye some food and drink."

The woman with a basket over her arm filled with cloths and jars moved past him and began to examine the lass. "Ainslee, ye will need to help me remove her clothes so she will be more comfortable. Plus, if she tumbled down the steps, she may have scraped herself in various places."

Callum turned and left the bedchamber and headed downstairs.

He had no idea who the lass was, but apparently with the fuss being made, she must be a family member. Perhaps wife to one of the Sutherland men.

After taking a seat at one of the long tables, a serving lass came by and asked what he wanted. He asked for anything that was hot and was pleased to receive a warm bowl of fragrant stew and fresh bread and butter. A large glass of ale washed it all down quite nicely.

It felt good to merely sit in the room. There were several older men gathered in a corner. They appeared to be playing a few games. And drinking their ale. Most likely warriors too old to train and fight.

During the half an hour that passed while Callum watched the men, he glanced occasionally toward the stairs, waiting for the laird to come down and formally toss him out. At least he would leave with a full belly and quenched thirst.

He also spent time considering the poor lass upstairs. Hopefully she wasn't badly injured, but head injuries could be dangerous. The sound of heavy footsteps drew his attention to the bottom of the stairs, as the laird moved toward him. The mon nodded at the lass clearing one of the tables. "An ale for me and one more for—" he hesitated, "—our guest." He added, "Who isna staying."

The laird remained silent for a few minutes until Callum was so edgy, he planned to just hop up and leave. Except he was concerned about the lass who fell. Finally, drawing on his strength and confidence as a mon and warrior, he said, "How is the lass?"

The Sutherland looked over at him. "I want to thank

ye for saving my sister, Donella, from more serious injuries by catching her when she fell. If it were not for ye, I am sure we would be planning the lass's funeral right now."

Callum nodded.

"What was so important for ye to speak with me that ye went through giving up yer armor—except for the knife tucked into the belt behind ye, hidden by yer leine and jerkin?"

Callum was not surprised the laird kenned he'd kept one weapon on him. The Sutherland didn't get the reputation he had by letting things like that slip.

He looked him in the eye and said, "I am offering my skills in exchange for a place in yer clan."

The laird crossed his arms over his chest, looking both curious and skeptical. "And what skills would that be?"

"I am a warrior. I have been trained by the best, worked as one of two seconds-in-command to my da, Laird Gunn, acquitted myself in many battles, and trained others in my clan."

Based on the laird's expression, Callum had a feeling this was no' going to get him a place in the clan. He should down the rest of his ale and be on his way. But one thing plagued him. "Ye dinna answer me before. How is the lass who fell down the stairs?"

The laird's demeanor immediately changed to one of concern. "She took quite a blow to her head. She also has some scrapes over her arms and legs."

"What does the healer say?" He had no idea why the lass's condition was important to him but in some way, he felt responsible for her.

He found her to be light as a feather in his arms as he

carried her up the steps. The scent of flowers surrounded him as he hurried down the corridor, following Lady Sutherland. Once he brought the lass to the bedchamber and laid her on the bed, he stared at her, her beauty taking his breath away.

The laird shrugged. "Our healer, Dorathia winna ken until Donella wakes up."

Callum rose and stepped away from the table. "Thank ye for yer time, Laird. I shall be on my way now."

"I doona remember dismissing ye." He nodded to the bench Callum had just moved away from. "Sit yerself back down and tell me why ye are not still a second-in-command to The Gunn?"

Another mug of ale appeared in front of him, and he took a sip. "I doona think it is generally keened yet, but my da was killed in a skirmish with the Mackays a short while back."

"That's a mighty large clan for ye clan to take on."

Callum shrugged. "We dinna start it. Well, not exactly. We had been doing a bit of reiving and they took offense to it."

The laird nodded for him to continue.

"My brother, Fraser swore to the clan that I fumbled during the battle, causing my da's death. He was so verra sure of himself that others in the clan believed him." He stopped and looked Haydon in the eye. "Twas not true. I was ne'er near him in the battle."

"What of those who were nearby? Dinna they see what happened?"

"Nay. Ye ken how a battle is. Ye doona see much of what's going with others around ye when yer trying to keep yer head attached to yer shoulders. I just kenned that during the entire—verra short—battle none of the men surrounding me from my clan, was my da."

The laird leaned forward, his forearms resting on his thighs. "So yer brother is now laird?"

"Aye. He's the oldest of the two of us, so I ne'er had reason to dispute him taking over the lairdship. That is the reason I doona understand why he made that accusation, and then did his best to turn the clan against me. After some time and a few scuffles between me and my men over this, my brother banned me from the clan."

"Wheest!" Haydon shook his head and sat back, crossing his arms over his chest. "Even if what he is saying is true—and I'm no' saying I believe it, I agree there seems no reason for him to go that far." He stopped and looked at him, the silence growing until Callum felt the need to shift in his seat, but dinna want to show that weakness.

"We ne'er take men from other clans, but since ye were so quick on yer feet that we dinna lose Donella—at least not yet—I will give ye a chance to prove yerself."

Callum nodded. Whatever the laird had in mind he was sure he could acquit himself. Until Haydon said, "Ye will face me on the lists."

Although his stomach dropped to his knees, he dinna show any reaction. Apparently the laird dinna want him to stay in his clan and intended to prove it. Facing the braw mon, with the reputation he had was a sure way to guarantee that Callum would be on his way before gloaming. Hopefully not missing any important body parts.

Haydon called for Callum's armor to be returned and they headed to the Lists. Somehow word had spread that the laird was going to challenge a member of the Gunn Clan.

Once they reached the Lists, Haydon stripped down to just his plaid and Callum did the same. Despite his concern about this battle, he was still aware of the looks and comments from some of the lasses who had gathered around them.

Callum flexed his muscles and rotated his neck. He wiped his palms on his plaid and picked up his sword. They faced each other in the cool early summer air. Knees bent, the circling began.

As expected, Haydon waited for Callum to make the first move. Which he did. Haydon hopped back, swung at Callum and the swords clashed. The power behind the laird's swing should have been expected, but it did take Callum a moment to re-think his attack.

They circled and swung, the swords clashing amid the sounds of the clan members cheering their laird on. The battle went on much longer than Callum had expected, but since he'd been without steady hot meals and little sleep, it was no surprise to him that he began to falter.

He put all his power into a swing and the laird moved quickly underneath Callum's sword and the weapon went flying. The laird rested the tip of his sword at Callum's neck. Both men were breathing heavily and Callum could feel blood dripping from his arm even though he'd ne'er realized he'd been cut.

The laird removed his sword from Callum's neck and slid it into the scabbard strapped to this back. Callum walked over and picked up his sword and slid it into the one by his side. "Shall I leave?"

Haydon placed his hands on his hips and stared at him for a moment and shook his head. "Nay. We could use yer skills."

Callum gave him a brief nod.

Haydon turned to one of the men in the circle surrounding them and said, "Take Gunn to the warrior's quarters and get him settled."

"Thank ye, my laird."

"Just so you ken, I will be sending a missive to yer brother to hear his side of yer story."

Callum kenned exactly what Fraser would say. He'd been blathering the false story since the battle that had felled Da. 'Twould be up to Haydon as to what side of the story he believed. As long as he now had a place to stay with the promise of work and hot meals, he would enjoy it as long as he could. Mayhap if he proved himself that would be enough to keep his place here.

The Sutherland clan was powerful and well-respected. Callum's clan, the Gunns was small and had always been at odds with their neighbors. With his laird allowing him to stay was proof enough that Sutherland had no fear of the Gunn Clan.

The mon Sutherland had directed to get him settled waved a hand at him. "I'm Hamish Sutherland. If the gossip is correct, ye are a Gunn and were banned from yer clan."

"Aye. Bad news travels fast. 'Tis true. Our laird is sending word to my brother, the new laird of Gunn, that I am here. We shall see what happens from that. All I will say to ye is there was a misunderstanding between me and my brother."

Hamish didn't question him further and walked them back to the outer bailey. "We generally take our meals and sleep in the great hall. There's a room at the back of the keep where ye can keep any personal items ye have."

Callum snorted. "What I own is what I'm wearing. I could use another set of clothes so I can at least wash these."

"Aye," Hamish said with a grin. "Ye do smell a tad foul. But I notice ye got a scratch during the clash with the laird. Ye best see Dorathia, our healer, and have her look at it. Ye doona want the cut to become infected."

They continued to walk to a small building at the back of the castle walls. The room was dark and obviously belonged to the warriors. Hamish waved his arm around. "When we're not walking the walls, training, eating, or asleep in the great hall, this is where we can take a moment to relax." He grinned again, the mon apparently being of the happy sort, "No' that there is any time to relax."

Once he showed him the small building, he said, "Come let us get Dorathia to look at yer wound, then I ken find a lass to rustle up some clothes for ye. The women are always making new ones since so many of ours end up in tatters after all the training we do." He waved in the southeast direction. "The loch behind us is generally where we get to smelling better."

Even though his place in the clan was not permanently guaranteed, Callum felt comfortable, needed, and settled for the first time in all the weeks since he'd left Gunn.

Next he had to figure out why Fraser had acted as he had.

3

---

*D*onella opened her eyes, which immediately filled with tears at the pain in her head. Verra slowly, she moved her head and looked across the room. She was in her bed but dinna remember why she was there and why her head hurt so verra much.

"Oh, thank the good Lord, Donella. Yer awake!" Every word of Ainslee's voice pounded in her head. "How do ye feel?" Her sister-by-marriage walked over to the bed.

"My head hurts like the devil. What happened to me?"

Rather than sit on the bed for which Donella was grateful because she kenned any movement would hurt her head even more, Ainslee took a seat on a chair next to the bed. "Ye fell down the stairs and knocked yerself out. Do ye no' remember?"

Donella started to shake her head but stopped the minute the pain intensified. "Nay. Can ye ask Dorathia to mix up a potion for me?"

"Aye, of course, lass. I'll go now."

TO CHARM A HIGHLANDER

Smart enough no' to nod again, Donella merely said in a very quiet voice, "Thank ye."

While Ainslee was gone, Donella closed her eyes which seemed to ease the pain a bit. Try as best she could, the fall down the stairs dinna appear in her memory. Of course, when something like that happens, 'tis so fast there really wasna much to remember.

One thing that did nudge at her thoughts was landing in the arms of a mon who had raced toward the stairs when she'd screamed. Most likely one of her brothers, but for some reason it dinna feel like Conall or Haydon when she landed.

She was verra tired but 'twas better if she saw Dorathia first and have her mix up a potion for her head. 'Twould also make her sleep, but the little bit she kenned from working with the healer occasionally, sleep was the best thing for the body after any sort of injury or illness.

The sound of the door opening made her realize she'd fallen asleep. "Lass, 'tis verra happy ye are awake." Haydon's booming voice almost split her head in two.

"Lower yer voice, husband. The lass has a verra bad headache." Ainslee followed the laird in with Dorathia right behind them, her ever-present basket over her arm.

"Aye, yer wife is correct, my laird. I'm sure Donella has one devil of a headache," Dorathia said as she gently set her basket on the bed. "Aside from yer headache, lass, is anything else bothering ye?"

"I have some pain on my arm and leg."

The healer nodded. "Aye, that is expected. Ye smacked the stairs when ye fell and scraped up your arm and leg." Gently, the healer slid her hand under Donella's head and felt the bump there. "Yer swelling has gone down a bit, and that is a good sign." She straightened up and looked at Haydon and Ainslee. "I think ye can stop yer worrying. The lass is young and healthy, and it appears now that she's awake, it's just a matter of time before she is on her feet again."

Ainslee let out a sigh of relief. "That is verra good news. Thank ye."

Dorathia nodded and pulled a jar out of her basket. "I will go to the kitchen and mix up a potion for the lass that will help her sleep."

Ainslee bent over and lightly kissed Donella's forehead. "Sleep well, sister, in no time at all ye will be feeling better."

Haydon gently laid his hand on her arm and smiled. "Ye need to heal fast, sister, the garden needs yer attention."

The garden? She dinna understand what he meant, but too tired to think about it, she closed her eyes and waited for Dorathia to return and give her the potion that would let her sleep.

Donella had been in bed, according to her calculations for five days and she was eager to be up and around. Today was the day Ainslee and Maura, Donella's cousin, Malcolm's wife, were to come to her bedchamber and help her dress and escort her downstairs to break her fast. She was anxious to see everyone again and eat a meal at the table.

She hadn't admitted to anyone, but her memory was giving her trouble. Some things came easy to her, like

TO CHARM A HIGHLANDER

who her family members were, but other things they spoke about left her confused. They treated her like a little girl, and it had become annoying. She certainly remembered she was three and twenty summers and wanted to shake off their concern which was becoming more like they were dealing with a bairn. Most likely once she was putting in a full day's work, they would ease up on their worry.

"Good morning, Donella," Maura said as she and Ainslee entered the room. Donella had a brief visit from her brothers and cousin, Malcolm, but as men were apt to be, they were anxious to say hello and then leave the sick room. The mon she was still wanting to see was the one who caught her in his arms when she fell down the stairs.

All she could remember were his deep green eyes and handsome face, twisted with alarm as she landed in his arms. Right after that she passed out and woke up the next day.

Once she was dressed and her hair fixed in a way that the still healing bruise on her head was hidden, the three women descended the stairs to the great hall. It took some bravery on Donella's part to place her foot on the step. Whether for her safety or their concern for her fear, the two women each took one of her arms as they made their way down.

It felt good to be on her feet again and the wonderful smells coming from the room had her stomach rumbling.

"A tad hungry, are ye lass?" Haydon walked up behind her, placing his hand on her shoulder. Conall stood alongside him. They all made their way to the dais to break their fast.

Donella looked around the room, happy that she had

no problem remembering, even though she was still plagued by some memory loss. Dorathia had assured her that it was something that would return in bits and pieces. What was interesting was the fact that she was quite happy with what she remembered and didn't feel the need to search for the missing pieces.

She thanked the lass who brought her a bowl of hot, wonderful-smelling porridge. As she slathered butter on a piece of warm bread, her eyes wandered the room. Then her movements stopped and she stared at the mon whose face she would ne'er forget.

'Twas the mon who saved her from certain death. As she stared at him, he turned almost as if he'd received a message from her. Their eyes met and Donella felt as though someone had set her body on fire.

"What is it, sister?" Conall said.

"That mon." She dinna want to point to him since he continued to watch her, a slight smile on his handsome face. "That is the one who saved me when I fell down the stairs."

"Aye," her brother said.

"He doona look familiar to me."

Conall took a sip of ale. "Nay."

"Who is he?"

"He's new. He arrived the day he caught you."

"Arrived from where?"

"Gunn."

"The clan?"

"Aye."

She huffed. "Christ's toes, brother, do I have to pull every word out of ye?"

Conall looked up at her from shoveling food into his mouth in surprise. Just then she noticed the others at their table were all looking at her. "What? Did I say something wrong? Why are ye all staring?"

Ainslee shook her head. "So sorry, lass, 'tis just ye usually speak much softer. I guess the bang on yer head raised yer voice."

Donella turned back to Conall. "Are ye going to tell me who the mon is, or will I have to wander over there and ask him?" She rolled her eyes. "Please close yer mouth brother, or ye will be catching midges."

Conall cleared his throat. "The mon is Callum Gunn. He had some problems with his clan and is staying here for a while."

She frowned. "Staying here for a while? What does that mean? What sort of a problem did he have?"

Again everyone at the table was glancing in her direction. Frustrated with all their nonsense, she dug into her food and decided to wait until the meal was over and then seek out the mon and thank him herself.

"Are ye well, sister?" Ainslee asked.

"Aye. 'Tis a good thing to be out of bed. However, I doona seem to remember which chores are mine. Ye mentioned something about the garden, but that slips my mind, also, as other things do. I'll be happy to look at it, though. I'll also be visiting Dorathia so I can learn some of the things she does to heal people. I think I'd like to train in the healing arts."

Now those at the table were no longer staring at her, but at each other. No one was speaking but they all looked verra confused. She shrugged and moved her chair back so she could catch Mr. Gunn before he left, she assumed, for the lists.

Conall grabbed her arm. "Where are ye going, lass?"

"To see Mr. Gunn. I want to thank him for saving my life. I assume that is acceptable to ye?" She looked at the others at the table. "Ye are all acting verra strange this morning." With those words she walked away and caught Mr. Gunn just as he rose to join the other men.

Again when he turned toward her she felt mesmerized, as if they had a connection. 'Twas probably because his face was the last thing she saw before she knocked herself unconscious.

"Good morning, Lady Donella. I am pleased to see ye looking well." His voice was everything his eyes were.

She had to swallow a few times to be able to speak. "I am well, Mr. Gunn. Thanks to ye. I ken I wouldn't be standing here now if it weren't for yer quick actions."

He moved his arm as if he planned to touch her, then dropped it to his side again. "'Twas worth saving ye, lass."

They both stood there, just looking at each other. Finally, he broke away from her gaze. "Well, I must be off to the lists."

She kenned better than to wander over to the lists later and watch him because one of her brothers, or both, would lock her in her bedchamber for disrupting the training.

He dinna seem any more eager to leave her than she was to let him go, which was silly since 'twas the first time they spoke to each other. She smiled and after a slight hesitation, he turned and walked from the room.

Donella returned to the table. "I am off to visit

Dorathia, unless there is something else ye need me for?" she asked Ainslee.

"Nay, lass. Ye can check the garden later since one of the kitchen lasses has been keeping it up while ye were not feeling well."

Again, Donella was confused about the garden. That was one memory she hadn't recalled.

4

Haydon, Ainslee, Conall, and Maura all stared at Donella as she walked—very confidently—over to where some of the men sat and engaged Gunn in conversation.

Haydon thought they must all look like idiots with their mouths hanging open. He noticed a few of the other clanfolk followed Donella with their eyes also. Everyone looked verra surprised.

"Whatever has happened to Donella?" Ainslee asked him.

He shrugged. "I have no idea. She's spent most of her life living like a shadow, trying verra hard to be invisible. How can a knock on the head change the lass's verra nature?"

Conall swung his gaze from Donella to his brother. "'Tis verra strange, for certes. She never spoke to me that way. I must admit, however, if this is a permanent change, I like it. She reminds me of the way she was when we were bairns. I remember her chasing after me to play with me and the other lads. Then she changed so much, and I never thought to see that lass again."

Donella headed back to them, and with every ounce of confidence she now possessed, told them she was going to be training with Dorathia. Four sets of eyes watched her stride from the great hall and leave the keep.

* * *

"Good morning, lass, 'tis verra good to see ye up and about. Ye had me worried there when the young warrior carried ye to yer bed."

Donella flushed at the healer's words. The thought of Gunn taking her to bed was verra interesting, but considering the mon had just arrived, 'twas not a good thing to be considering. She must learn from Haydon what the mon's status was and if his stay here was, in fact, temporary. 'Twas annoying that Conall would give her no more information.

"I am feeling quite well, Dorathia. Thank ye so much for yer attention. The healing draughts ye gave me helped a great deal."

"What can I do for ye this morning? Not feeling pain in yer head again, are ye?"

"No. The reason I came is I would like to train with ye. While ye were attending me, it seemed like something I would verra much like to do."

Dorathia's eyes grew wide. "Do ye meant that, lass?"

Donella frowned. "Aye, I do."

"'Tis verra good news. I've been trying to get ye to take an interest in healing, but ye always shied away."

She shrugged. "I doona ken why. I think 'twould be verra interesting and helpful.'"

"Then, let's go over some things that ye need to ken to begin the healing process for most injuries, which we see many of here due to the warriors always swinging at each other and the bairns running around crashing into things."

Donella grinned. "Or lasses tumbling down the stairs."

Dorathia looked oddly at her, but then grinned. "Aye, lass. Tumbling down the stairs."

Just then a mon ran through Dorathia's door. "Dorathia, ye must come. My wife believes the bairn is about to be born."

Donella recognized Rory Sutherland, whose wife, Sorcha, of less than a year was nearing her time. She turned to Dorathia. "What shall I do?"

The healer spewed out instructions on what they needed to bring with them. When they were about halfway packed and ready, Dorathia said to her, "Go to the stable and have two horses readied for us."

Rory had already left as soon as he'd seen the women packing things up. The poor mon looked verra nervous. Childbirth was indeed risky. Donella hurried to the stablemaster, Angus, Jonet's son, who had taken over the spot from Broderick when the old stablemaster passed away the year before.

Panting for breath, she said, "Dorathia and I need two horses."

Angus stared at her.

"What is it? We need two horses."

The young mon shook his head. "'Tis sorry I am, lass, ye just startled me."

She stood tapping her foot while Angus made two horses ready. She smiled at him to make up for any annoyance she'd shown before. "Thank ye."

She took the reins from him as he continued to stare at her and walked the horses to the front of the keep. People were certainly acting verra unusual since she'd recovered from her injury. Mayhap they believed she wouldna recover and were surprised to see her up and moving.

* * *

TAKING A SHORT BREAK FROM TRAINING, Callum poured a bucket of water over his head. The coolness felt good after the sweat he'd worked up. As he put the bucket down, his attention was taken up with two women hurrying toward waiting horses, both loaded down with bundles. He recognized the older woman as Dorathia, the healer who had bustled into Lady Donella's bedchamber after he'd laid her on the bed the day she took a tumble down the keep stairs.

The other lass was Lady Donella herself. He was once again mesmerized by the beauty that didn't even begin to describe her. She had an aura of the fairies about her, something that caught his entire insides and twisted him into knots. He was stunned when she'd marched over to him after he broke his fast to thank him for saving her.

For days, he'd been listening to tales from the other warriors of how simple-minded Lady Donella was. That she acted like a bairn and her brother had given up on arranging a marriage for her years ago. The general opinion throughout the castle was Lady Donella was verra, verra strange.

'Twas no' a strange lass who approached him this morning. She was beautiful, with her flowing brown hair, loosely tied at her nape. Her blue eyes were the color of a cloudless sky. She was friendly and had a verra intelligent look in her eyes. It appeared her own clan dinna even ken the lass well at all.

Just then Malcolm came jogging up to him. "The laird requests ye attend him in his solar."

Shaking his head to clear some of the water out, Callum ran his fingers through his hair as he made his way to the keep. He felt as though he'd settled in quite well and hoped the laird was not about to give him bad news. Since the Gunn Clan bordered the Sutherlands, there was a good chance he'd already received a response from Fraser, and it was now that he'd be asked to pack up and go.

He sighed. Sutherland was a fine clan, and if he couldna be a part of his own clan, he'd hoped to stay here. The men were friendly, they fought together well, and he saw none of the nasty competitiveness among the men that was so prevalent in his clan. He'd often spoken to his da about it, but he seemed to enjoy seeing the men wrangle with each other. On the other hand, Callum felt they should be more of a team, loyal to each other, rather than looking to cut each other down.

He was quite certain Fraser was running the warriors the same way since he had sided with their da when the discussions had come up.

Inside the keep was cool, which chilled him considering that he'd just dumped a bucket of water over his head. He made his way up the stairs to the second level and down the corridor until he reached the laird's solar. He knocked once and was granted entrance.

As he'd assumed, a piece of parchment lay on the laird's desk. "Have a seat, Gunn."

Callum sat, his elbows resting on the arms of the large wooden chair, his fingers linked in front of him. Everything in the laird's solar was large, just like the mon himself. He could tell nothing from The Sutherland's expression. He might have been summoned to be ordered to leave, or to tell him he was to marry his sister. Just the thought of having the beautiful Donella in his bed was enough to have him shifting around in his chair. 'Twas more likely he was being asked to pack his things and be on his way. He was certainly no' good enough for Lady Donella.

Haydon tapped the piece of parchment on his desk. "I have one question for ye, Gunn."

"Aye?"

"Why does yer brother hate ye so?"

Although he'd felt it, 'twas quite a surprise to hear the laird ask that question.

Rather than play games and pretend he dinna ken what the laird was asking him, he merely shrugged his shoulders. "I have no idea, Laird. 'Twas not that way when we were bairns. We played together all the time. Then for some reason, Fraser turned against me."

The Sutherland nodded and tapped the parchment again. "He says here just what ye told me, about ye fumbling in battle and causing yer da's death. If what ye say is the truth, why do ye believe he is spreading that story?"

"I doona ken. I see no benefit in it. I should be his second-in-command. He always trusted me in battle and relied on me to train the men." Callum shrugged. "'Tis a mystery to me."

Callum sat for a minute, watching the laird read the note over again. Finally, he looked up. "Ye are a good warrior, Gunn. Good with yer sword and yer knives. Malcom and Conall both tell me ye would be a fine addition to our clan." He leaned back, his hands placed face down on the desk. "I doona ken why yer brother would say such a thing, but since we've had time to watch ye and from what the other men have told me, I see no reason to ask ye to leave. But if ye stay, be aware, we expect yer loyalty. Should for some reason we end up in a battle against the Gunn's allies, or the Gunns themselves, I expect ye to fight as a Sutherland."

Callum nodded. "I would expect no less, my laird. I appreciate yer faith in me and I willna let ye down."

Hayden nodded back. "Then I expect ye to swear yer loyalty."

Callum stood and moved to where the laird sat. He knelt on one knee, bowed his head and swore his loyalty.

He stood and left the solar, relief flooding him. 'Twas not an easy thing for a mon to be banned from his clan, especially when the clan laird was yer own brother.

He might ne'er understand what Fraser's motives were, or what he hoped to gain by spreading such a story, but for now he was just grateful to have a place to lay his head and hot food to eat.

He opened the keep door and was smacked in the chest by a soft, warm body. He looked down at Lady

Donella, her face flushed, out of breath. He took her by the arms. "Are ye well, lass?"

She placed her hand on her chest, trying to steady her breathing. "Aye. I was sent by Dorathia for something we forgot when we went to Sorcha's bedside."

She started to walk past him, but he walked alongside her until they reached a small cottage in the corner of the inner bailey. "Can I help ye?"

"Nay. 'Tis childbirth."

She grinned when he gulped and flushed. "'Tis true, lass. I canna help ye."

He hated to see her rush off like this. He would love to spend some time with her. No one seemed to think she was betrothed to anyone. Although, based on what he'd heard over the past week, 'twas everyone's opinion she would ne'er marry because she was simple-minded.

"Then I wish ye and Dorathia luck, Lady Donella. I hope yer patient does well."

She fumbled through a basket on a shelf and pulled something out. When she started past him again, he said, "Do ye have a horse to carry ye?"

"Aye, I do." She stopped and looked up at him, her eyes bright with life. "I will tell Sorcha ye wish her well." She seemed to hesitate for a moment, but then realizing she had been sent for something needed for childbirth, she turned and hastened to the horse waiting for her by the gate.

She grinned at him and waved as she turned the horse and rode off.

5

Donella continued to believe her plan of assisting Dorathia and learning the healing arts under her guidance was a good one, but wasna too sure about childbirth. Luckily, Dorathia's niece, Helena, had taken o'er that part of the work for the clan, but she'd been visiting her sister who'd married a Mackay and had just given birth to her first bairn. Once she returned Donella would be more than happy to hand over that part of Dorathia's work to her.

For more than fifteen hours the poor mother had suffered. Donella had to finally go back to the keep and ask Malcolm or Conall to take Rory in hand since he was making things more difficult for the women with his constant asking if e'erthing was well and when would the bairn arrive.

Since both men had suffered through this before, they were happy to get the mon away from his house and to the keep where they told her they would ply him with enough whisky to calm him, but not too much to pass out.

TO CHARM A HIGHLANDER

. . .

DONELLA WAS RETURNING to the keep, dragging her exhausted body after hours of watching poor Sorcha scream, threaten to slice Rory's prideful part from his body, and push, push, push.

Childbirth was indeed a painful, messy, noisy event. She thought back to all her years since she'd become of marriageable age and wondered for the first time why Haydon had ne'er arranged a marriage for her. Based on what she kenned about her sisters-in-law, by now Donella should be married with a few bairns pulling at her skirts. She must ask the laird about that after she treated her body to several hours of sleep.

"Lady Donella, yer are looking lovely as always, but certainly worn out. I assume ye just finished with the childbirth ye were rushing off to when I saw ye last?" Callum Gunn walked up to her from behind, most likely just leaving the lists and heading to the great hall for the noon meal.

The sweat on his body caused his leine to cling to him, making the garment transparent. His bulging muscles as he moved did strange things to her insides. She'd seen men leaving the lists for years, but ne'er noticed, or e'en cared what they looked like under their leines.

"Aye," she smiled, answering his question. "A fine lad. Healthy and with a strong voice. Rory and Sorcha are verra happy." She laughed. "At least Sorcha is no longer threatening to cut off Rory's..." She blushed and Callum laughed.

"Ouch, lass, 'tis painful just to hear such words."

They strolled along for a few minutes, then Callum

said, "I assume ye will be taking yer meal before ye fall into bed?"

There was that word again. Why did 'bed' always seem to be part of their conversation? "Aye. I need to clean up first."

"I've seen that the nooning is less formal than supper. Can I ask ye to join me?" He hurried on. "No' at the warriors' table with all the other men. Maybe one near the front of the room where yer brothers can see us."

Donella smiled brightly despite her fatigue. "Aye, Mr. Gunn. I would like that."

He made a face. "Please call me Callum. I doona want ye to think of myself so formally."

She dipped her head. "Then you must call me Donella. Lady Donella sounds too formal to me, as well."

He nodded. "After I clean up too, I will meet ye in the great hall." He opened the door, and the smell of a wonderful soup or stew greeted them. Both of their stomachs rumbled at the same time, and they grinned at each other.

* * *

Donella felt as though she was floating on air. Her tiredness diminished once Callum asked her to join him for the nooning meal. He was the first mon to ever pay attention to her. For years everyone, no' just the men, avoided her, which now made her wonder why. Her reflection in the looking glass told her she was no' a bad looking lass.

He was a handsome mon, too. Verra tall, broad shouldered with dark curly hair that kept falling onto his forehead. His locks were lengthy, held back with a piece of leather. But Callum's main feature was his deep green eyes. Eyes that she'd seen in her dreams when she was recovering from her head injury.

"Something has ye looking quite cheerful," Maura said as Donella passed her in the corridor.

"Aye. 'Tis been a long night. Sorcha and Rory Sutherland welcomed a lad into their home today."

Maura's eyebrows rose. "Aye? 'Tis wonderful." She hesitated for a moment. "Ye were there, then?"

"Aye. I want to learn Dorathia's healing arts, but with Helena visiting her sister at the Mackay's I helped her today with the birth."

Her sister-in-law stared at her. "Ye did? How…interesting." She stumbled over the last word.

Donella's smile dimmed. What was wrong with everyone? She shook her head and continued on her way. Once she was cleaned up and changed into fresh garments, she laughed at herself when she pinched her cheeks and bit her lips. She'd seen Maura and Ainslee do so when they were meeting up with their husbands.

Husband. Something her brother had apparently not concerned himself with. Mayhap because she was his only sister, and he was unsure how to handle it. Then she laughed out loud. There wasna anything Haydon Sutherland dinna ken how to handle.

Callum awaited her in the great hall. He had also cleaned up, but since he would be returning to the lists after nooning, he hadn't changed his clothes.

He walked up to her and offered a slight bow. "You are looking lovely, my lady."

Donella flushed and grinned. "And you are looking well yourself."

He waved her forward and they chose a table near the dais where Haydon, Ainslee, Conall, Maura, Malcolm and Christine sat. E'en though Malcolm lived in his own house on property given to him by Haydon when he married Christine, he still appeared at the lists every day to help with the training of the warriors.

Donella smiled as she watched all the ladies wrestle with bairns on their laps. Once she had settled into her seat, she felt the need to stamp her foot at the looks she was receiving from her family. Christ's toes, whatever was wrong with them?

Perhaps she hadn't received attention from men before, but she was now, and she intended to enjoy it.

Within minutes, the young serving lasses came from the kitchen with bowls of fragrant stew, loaves of warm bread and freshly churned butter.

* * *

HAYDON LEANED OVER TO AINSLEE, trying his best to speak low enough, but over his daughter, Grace's enthusiastic babbling. "What do ye think about the change in Donella?"

His wife shrugged. "I doona have any idea. But whate'er caused the change, I am delighted with it."

"Do ye think a knock on the head can change a person's nature?" he asked.

"There is so little we ken about the body, especially the mind." Ainslee shuffled Grace from her lap onto Haydon's since the lass was extending her little arms out toward her da.

Haydon tugged his hair from his daughter's chubby fist. "I ne'er thought about finding a husband for the lass since she appeared uninterested in such things."

"As well as most things. But if this new behavior continues, she might be ready for a husband and a family."

The laird looked over to where Donella and Gunn were chattering away as if they'd kenned each other for years instead of a few days.

"She seems to like the new warrior," Ainslee said.

Haydon frowned. "Aye. And he seems to like her as well."

Grace stood on Haydon's thighs and began to bounce. "But I still doona trust the mon completely."

"Has he given ye reason to no' trust him?"

The laird studied his sister and the mon. "It still causes me to wonder why his brother was so free to loss the mon out of his clan. 'Tis usually a serious reason to do such a thing. From what I've seen so far, nothing about the mon deserves such treatment."

Conall leaned toward Haydon on his other side. "Are ye thinking what I'm thinking, brother?"

"What is that?" He placed Grace on his shoulders as she continued to yank on his hair. He would be bald by the time his bairns were all grown.

"'Tis time ye found a husband for Donella. Whatever the problem has been mayhap the whack on her head knocked it out of her."

Haydon sighed. "I need to speak with Dorathia. I dinna ken if she has any more ideas than we do—which is none, but as much as I love the change in the lass, something in me says 'tis not permanent."

"That is a verra negative opinion, brother."

He grabbed Grace as she began to fall backward. "Mayhap I'm merely preparing myself for a disappointment."

* * *

"I DOONA care for the way yer brother watches us," Callum said to Donella as he observed the laird from under shuttered eyelashes.

"He's been acting verra strange since I recovered from my fall." Donella stabbed a piece of meat in the trencher and slipped it into her mouth. "He behaves as though he doona ken me."

Silent for a moment, Callum said, "Why isna a lass as beautiful as ye married? Or did ye lose yer husband in a battle?"

Donella swallowed a piece of bread and licked her lips. She glanced over at Callum who was looking at her in a strange way. Christ's toes, not him too. "I canno' say for sure. I doona remember exactly what my life was like before I fell. Everything is muddled. It seems to me I spent a great deal of time walking in the woods at the back of the castle."

"I thought ye worked with Dorathia?"

She shook her head. "Nay. I am enjoying my time with her and canno' understand why I dinna work with her before now. Ainslee said something about returning to my work in the garden, but I remember doing that when my mam was alive. I donna recall that after she died."

After a few moments of silence, Callum cleared his throat. Donella looked over at him. He gave her a slight grin. "Do ye think ye would want to take a trip to the village with me sometime?"

She smiled back. "Aye, I would like that."

"I think I should ask the laird for his permission."

Well, then. It appeared Callum Gunn was truly interested in her. Despite the fatigue she'd been fighting since leaving Rory's home earlier with the sweet couple admiring their new bairn, she felt her spirits rise. "Aye, that is probably a good idea."

Donella wiped her eating knife and slid it back into the small case at her waist, the little bit of boost she'd received from Callum's attention slowly fading as her fatigue returned. "I think I will leave ye now. I need to get some sleep before my head drops into my trencher."

Callum stood as she did. "Do ye want me to walk ye up the stairs? Not that I think ye canno' do it, but ye are somewhat weary."

She smiled at his concern. "Thank ye, but I am sure I will be fine." She turned back when she reached the bottom of the stairs to see Callum aproaching Haydon at the dais.

6

As Callum reached the laird, with the family watching him carefully, he felt almost as if he faced another warrior on the battlefield.

Despite his nervousness, he was determined to gain Haydon's approval of him escorting Donella to the village. He looked Haydon straight in the eye and cleared his throat. "My laird, I seek permission to escort Lady Donella to the village for a short visit."

"Nay."

Callum was stunned at the laird's immediate and negative response. He felt the blood rush to his face and decided he would no' simply walk away. "May I ask why no', my laird?"

"Donella feels safer when she is closer to home."

Callum shook his head, unable to believe the laird's answer. "Excuse me, my laird, but you sound as though the lass is a bairn. Since I am one of your skilled warriors and ye trust me to defend ye castle, why would ye think Lady Donella would no' be safe with me?"

Haydon glanced over at his wife with an obvious look of confusion, seeming to beg for help.

Ainslee cleared her throat. "Do ye have reason to believe she would be receptive to the idea of a trip to the village with ye?"

"Aye, I would. I asked her already and she was verra excited about the idea."

Ainslee looked back at Haydon. "What is yer objection, my laird?"

"Ach. Ye must think this serious if yer calling me 'my laird.'" He studied Callum for a moment, then turned back to his wife. "Ye ken why, wife. Donella has ne'er been farther than the castle walls."

Lady Sutherland shrugged. "Mayhap she is ready for a change. Ye ken we've seen a change in yer sister. I'm thinking 'tis time to let her go, let her decide what she thinks is best for her."

Conall shook his head. "I doona like it either. Mayhap we can send some guards with them."

Callum growled. "Do ye intend to send guards with me when we go into battle? Am I so weak as to no' be able to take care of one lass?" He tried hard, but he kenned he was becoming quite angered and 'twas showing in his voice.

Ainslee placed her hand on Haydon's arm, apparently keeping him from flying across the table and pummeling him.

Maura spoke up for the first time. "I think ye are both being ridiculous. Christ's toes, let the lass go into the village with the mon. As he said, as one of yer warriors, he can certainly take care of Donella."

After a slight hesitation, the laird nodded. As he

opened his mouth to speak, his wife covered his hand with hers and when he looked at her, she shook her head.

Before one of the brothers spoke again, Callum nodded his head, bowed, and left the dais.

* * *

THE NEXT AFTERNOON Donella verra carefully descended the steps in the keep. Callum met her at the bottom and smiled brightly. He had cleaned up from his morning on the lists and looked verra handsome.

He took Donella's hand and intertwined their arms together as they left the keep. "Ye brothers are verra protective of ye, lass."

She sighed. "I ken. I doona understand it."

"Have they always been that way?"

"I'm not sure. I doona remember, but it seems to me I've forgotten some things since I knocked myself out. But from the way everyone has been treating me, it appears I must be somewhat different from how I was before." She shrugged.

"Well, Donella, I like the way ye are, so whatever changes they're seeing are certainly for the best."

The village was close enough that they decided to walk. It was a clear day, warm enough that her wrap was enough to keep her comfortable as they strolled along.

"What's yer favorite place to visit?" Callum asked as they reached the edge of the village.

Donella shrugged. "I'm no' sure. The last time I remember visiting the village was I went with my mam."

"Ye haven't been here since yer were a child?"

Donella frowned for a moment. "'Tis true. I doona

remember coming to the village since Mam passed away." She felt a tad agitated, as though she should have remembered something important, but then Callum took her hand in his and wrapped his arm around her.

"Doona fret. It dosna matter. Let's just enjoy our time today."

She shrugged it off as no' important. "Aye, there is so much to see." She inhaled deeply. "And a lot of wonderful things to taste."

It was quite obvious she hadn't been in the village for a long time. But rather than troubling herself about it, she enjoyed the fine weather, the handsome man by her side and the enthusiasm she felt with every store they visited and every vendor displaying their wares.

"Lady Donella!" A large woman most likely in her fiftieth year, waved at her. She looked familiar, but Donella wasna sure who she was. She walked toward her and offered a smile since the woman was smiling at her.

"'Tis so good to see ye, lass."

Donella continued to smile. "Aye, 'tis good to see ye as well."

"I must say all the stories we've heard about ye were certainly false. Ye are looking wonderful." She nudged Donella. "'Tis time to get married and get a few bairns, aye?"

The woman who Donella still didn't identify looked over at Callum. "'Tis yer job, young mon." She winked and thankfully, her attention was taken up by someone who wanted to purchase one of the warm Scottish scarves she was selling.

They walked a few more minutes, then Donella looked

at Callum. "I'm so sorry she said that. By the truth, I am getting quite confused."

The look on his face told her he understood her dilemma. "Is it possible lass, that there is part of yer memory missing since ye hit yer head?"

She sighed. "I doona ken. All my family members are acting strange, almost as if my entire person has changed." Suddenly, tears flooded her eyes and she looked at him, clinging to his arm. "I am becoming frightened, Callum."

"Mayhap it's time to confront Haydon and ask him for information. As yer laird and brother, he should put yer mind at ease."

She nodded. "But what if it is something disturbing. Something that my mind has blocked out? 'Twill for certes not ease my mind."

"Then ye have two choices, lass. Ask ye brother to tell ye what ye want to ken or put it all aside and enjoy this new life that everyone seems happy to see and ye seem content with."

"Aye, but am I content? How would ye feel if ye suffered a knock on the head and when ye opened yer eyes, ended up in a different life?"

"Lass, you doona ken if this is a different life. There is always the possibility that ye were more on the shy side and dinna enjoy visiting the village."

When she said nothing as she tried to make sense of it all, he added, "It appears ye are becoming addled over it, and it might not mean anything. What say ye we go to the alehouse and have a few sips. Mayhap a meat pie, also."

Things might have gone well had they no' been stopped a few times more by villagers remarking on how well she looked and what a surprise to see her out and about.

* * *

Callum was becoming concerned himself. The battle he had to fight her family to allow them to even travel to the village had been strange enough, but all these villagers who seemed to treat Donella as if she'd risen from the dead was frightening to him, even. What if the bump on her head had caused some type of memory loss? Was such a thing even possible?

For certes, with how happy everyone seemed to see her, he could only assume whatever the change had been, it had improved her life.

They entered the busy alehouse and found two seats at a table near the door. Donella was still looking uneasy, and he hoped a bit of ale, some food and instead of returning to the village a walk along the creek on the return home would soothe her.

"What are ye doing here? This isna where ye belong." A large mon, one who Callum couldn't even see since his body blocked the sunlight from the opened doorway, approached their table just as the young serving lass put their drinks down.

"Aye, 'tis me, Callum Gunn. And as ye can see, the lass and I are having a bite to eat. I must say that as much as I enjoy yer welcome, I canno' see yer face."

Gerard Gunn, a relation to him somewhere down the line, grabbed one of the chairs at their table, turned it around and straddled it, his large forearms resting on the back of the chair.

Callum studied the mon. "It appears to me that ye are the one with an answer of why a trip onto Sutherland land?"

Gerard turned to a table with two other men who apparently were with him and smirked. "I see no reason why we canna visit the village on Sutherland land. 'Tis no' as if our clans are at war."

He reached over and took a sip of Callum's ale and said, "Ah, so once yer brother tossed yer cowardly arse out of the clan, this is where ye ended up? Are ye married to the lass here, or is she up for grabs?"

Donella stiffened as she carefully placed her ale mug on the table. "I am no' married, and I am no' up for grabs."

Gerard threw his head back and laughed. "Aye, Callum, ye got yerself an spunky one here. Surely, someone as cowardly as yerself couldna handle such a woman." He reached out for Donella who pulled her arm away from his grip.

He grinned and looked back over at the table of men with him. "Ach, look who he has with him, trying to tup? The crazy Sutherland lass. I thought they locked her away years ago."

Donella sucked in a deep breath at the same time that Callum pushed his chair back so far, it slid halfway across the room. Before speaking a word, he grabbed Gerard around the throat and squeezed.

A trained warrior also, Gerard reached for his sword, which he dropped as Callum drew him away from the table so as not to injure Donella. Her screams in the background reached his ears as he and Gerard landed on the floor and continued to pummel each other.

"Stop!" From the side, he saw her grab a chair,

swinging it in their direction when one of the men with Gunn yanked the chair off her and wrapped his arm around her waist from behind.

Enraged further with Donella entrapped in the mon's arms, Callum pulled the dirk from his side and plunged it into Gerard's chest. It dinna stop the mon from his attack, but it slowed him down. Enough that Callum wrenched himself free from Gerard's grip, stood and kicked the mon in the head, knocking him out.

Without taking a breath, he swung at the mon holding Donella, knocking him to the ground.

The sound of a string of curse words sure to get the mon straight into hell, an awakened Gerard climbed back up to his feet and swung at Callum, his dirk in his hand.

A sting in his arm told Callum kenned he'd been stabbed, but in the middle of the brawl, he dinna even stop to consider it. He shook his head, grateful when another Sutherland joined the fray. Soon it appeared the entire room was filled with men rolling on the floor, blood, grunts, and shouting.

The ale house owner and two of his sons threw buckets of ice cold water from the nearby creek over the men rolling on the floor, which stopped the battle almost as fast as it had started.

Alehouse owner, Henry Sutherland, somewhere in his fiftieth years stood with his hands on his hips, breathing heavy as his two sons pulled the brawlers from the floor and shoved them toward the door.

Callum stumbled over to Donella. "Are ye well, lass? Did anyone hurt ye?" All he could think was Haydon was going to strip him of his skin.

Wide-eyed, she stared at his arm. "Nay, but it appears ye dinna miss getting yerself sliced up."

'Twas then that Callum felt the throb in his arm where Gerard's dirk had sliced him. It appeared he'd lost some blood, based on the rivulet running down his arm and pooling at his feet.

"I think 'tis best to get ye back to the Keep, Callum." Donella wrapped her arm around his waist to steady him. 'Twas ridiculous that he couldna fell the Gunn without getting hurt himself. A poor showing for a warrior, but since he wasna prepared to do battle while quietly sitting with Donella and even less wanting to kill the mon and start a war between the Gunns and the Sutherlands, 'twas for the best that it had ended as it had.

Although he continued to hush Donella from fussing at him all the way back to the keep, as she continued to attempt to secure a wagon to get them back, he had to admit he was feeling weaker with each step.

'Twould be humiliating enough to face her brothers after becoming injured while trying to defend their sister, but worse than that would be to collapse at their feet when they arrived.

"Someone help Cullum to a bedchamber upstairs and find Dorathia," Donella shouted as they reached the outer bailey.

"Lass, stop, please. I doona want the entire castle to learn of my disgrace. And I doona belong upstairs."

Just then one of the vassals hurried over. "What is the problem, Lady Donella?"

"Mr. Gunn has been injured." She looked over at Callum whose head was drooping. "He will need care after the injury is taken care of. He canna go to the warriors quarters."

Not having the strength to fight her again on where they were to lay his broken body, he dinna object. They summoned a mon passing by with a bundle over his shoulders and with the three of them, they got Callum upstairs to the bedchamber closest to the stairs.

She continued to assist holding him up. As much as he wanted to push away from her, he was fairly certain he would indeed suffer the ultimate humiliation and collapse.

He was dragged up the stairs and then deposited onto a soft bed right before everything went black.

* * *

Donella breathed a sigh of relief when Dorathia rushed into the room. "Is this one of the warriors, my lady?"

"Aye. Thank ye for coming so quickly."

The healer looked down at Callum. "Is this the Gunn warrior?"

"Aye. We were visiting the village and one of the Gunn warriors said something about me Callum took objection to, and a fight began."

Dorathia glanced in her direction as she removed items from her basket. "Ye went to the village?"

"Aye." After a minute of watching Dorathia examine the cut on Callum's arm and tsking, Donella said, "The few people we met in the village seemed surprised to see me. In fact, the way this fight started was when the Gunn warrior said he thought my family had locked me up years ago."

Dorathia looked over at her and said nothing, just continued her work.

"What do ye think about that, Dorathia?"

"Hand me a clean cloth from that pile over there." The healer nodded in the direction of a stack of linens. Apparently she wasna going to answer her question. Finally, when Donella had given up on gaining information, Dorathia said. "I think 'tis best if ye ask the laird if ye have questions."

If she hadn't been so concerned about Callum, she would have badgered Dorathia until she received some answers, but the look of the slice on his arm worried her.

"'Tis a good thing the young mon was brought back quickly. Also, 'tis a clean cut, so sewing it up won't be hard. He will be unable to do much in the way of practicing on the lists for a while, but aside from a fever, which I expect him to develop, as a young, strong mon he should recover just fine."

Donella was surprised at the relief she felt at the healer's words. Yes, she and Callum had become friends, but her reaction was more than one would have to hear good news about just a friend. Did that mean she was beginning to have feelings for the warrior? Feelings that could develop into something else? Something stronger?

That was another thing she intended to ask Haydon about. She had seen twenty-three summers. Why hadn't a marriage been arranged for her? Was it possible she had been married and her husband killed? In battle?

'Twould be no more wondering for her. Once Callum was settled, she would find Haydon, hopefully not on the lists since she couldna disturb him there.

With the patient asleep from the draught Dorathia had

given him after cleaning the wound and sewing him up, Donella headed down the stairs—still careful of where she stepped—and visited five different places before she found Haydon.

Her brother was in the stables, giving his five-year-old daughter, Susana a riding lesson. Donella found it interesting and touching to see how her growling, arrogant brother was so soft and gentle with his little lass.

It was apparently the end of their lesson, since Haydon lifted Susana from the horse and patted her on the head as she made her way back to the keep.

"Good afternoon, sister."

Donella smiled at him, always amazed at how he kenned who and what was in his surroundings at all times.

"Did ye enjoy yer trip to the village?" He slapped the horse on the rear, and the stable master took the beast to his stall.

"Aye, 'twas all right, but dinna end well."

Haydon's head jerked up and he looked Donella in the eyes. "What happened?"

"I'd rather speak with ye about another subject. Or perhaps my questions are related to how the trip to the village ended."

Haydon crossed his arms over his chest and stared at her. "Ye are speaking in riddles, sister."

"Nay. I'm beginning to believe my life is a riddle."

When he didn't respond, but kept staring at her, she said, "What is wrong with me, brother? I believe 'tis something everyone kens except me."

7

Haydon kenned this question was coming once they'd all seen the change in his sister. But with so little information himself, would it help or hurt Donella to learn what they did ken?

"Let us retire to my solar." As they began to walk, he said, "Before we begin this conversation, what happened at the village that made your visit no' end well?"

"Callum and I went to the ale house and a mon from the Gunn clan insulted me. I'm afraid Callum took a bad slice in his arm defending me. Dorathia just finished sewing him up."

She glanced over at him when he growled. "Before ye get any more upset, ye should ken that I had Callum put into one of the bedchambers. I dinna think he would get much care in the warrior quarters."

Haydon's brows rose. "Ye did, did ye? And since when do ye make decisions without consulting yer laird?"

She waved him off like a pesky insect. "By the time I

would have been able to find ye, the mon would have bled to death."

He was no longer stunned by the things Donella did and said since her head injury. He'd asked Dorathia many times if her memory would come back and the answer was always the same. She dinna ken and had no idea if it was permanent or no'.

What disturbed him most was they all kenned something happened to her when she was younger that changed her from a sweet, joyful lass into a shell of a person.

They were both caught up in their own thoughts as they made their way back to the keep and then up the stairs to his solar. No matter how many ways he thought of telling what she wanted to ken, the more confused he became. 'Twould be best to let her question him and tell her as much as he kenned.

Haydon had been stopped a few times on their journey. Donella seemed impatient as he was addressed by servants with troubles and a warrior wondering where Callum was since he'd heard the mon had been injured but wasna' in the warrior quarters. Making it sound as though it had been Dorathia's decision, he brushed the mon off before he could ask any more questions.

Once they were settled, with Haydon behind his desk and Donella sitting in the chair in front of him, she said, "Ever since I hit my head in the fall down the stairs, everyone has been acting strange."

Before he said something that would make matters worse, he asked, "What do ye mean by strange?"

She sighed. "Whatever I do, or say, or wherever I go, someone seems surprised to see me or almost shocked to hear what I say. I kenned that the fall hadn't changed my looks because I already asked Dorathia that question."

Haydon studied her for a minute. He and Ainslee had discussed this situation at length, and the only conclusion they came to was something happened to Donella around her fourteenth summer that had changed her into the quiet, almost strange lass she'd been up until her fall down the stairs.

"Do ye remember anything about yer fourteenth summer?"

Donella shrugged. "Nothing in particular."

He leaned his forearms on the desk and looked her in the eyes. 'Twas time to tell her what he kenned. He hoped it would not destroy the lass.

"You went missing that summer."

"Missing? What do ye mean?"

"Missing for a few days, even though it seemed longer to us. Da had died only a few months before and I was wrestling with problems as the new laird."

"How long, brother?"

"Four days. Ye were found wandering in the woods outside the castle walls. Ye refused to tell anyone where ye had been and what happened to ye."

Donella sat verra still, putting fear in Haydon that she'd remembered and once again returned to the state she'd been in since that had happened.

Eventually, she said. "I remember naught."

"Ye spent a lot of time with Mam doing gardening, but also wandered off—within the castle walls—for at least a part of every day. Ye seemed to be in a dream state.

"After a while, especially after Mam died, we just left ye to do what you wanted to do. Ye were responsible for the keep upon Mam's passing, but ye dinna have the will, it seemed, to do anything but draw on parchment and walk in the woods."

"Draw? I doona remember drawing."

They remained silent for a few minutes, Haydon watching Donella to see if anything came back to her mind that would upset her.

Nothing.

She sat with her hands folded in her lap and looked at them.

"Donella?" he said softly.

She smiled and looked up at him. "I am well, brother. I doona ken what happened those four days. Do ye recall what condition I was in when I was found?"

Did he remember? He would never forget it as long as he lived. The poor lass was filthy, her clothes torn. Upon examination she also had bruises on her body, obviously from a beating. Based on Dorathia's examination his sister had also been violated as well as everything else.

With her refusing to acknowledge what happened, it left Haydon and Conall with no way to find whoever had been responsible for Donella's condition.

They'd spent days going through the woods surrounding the castle, but found nothing and no one.

It was only after Mam's death that they realized she wasn't keeping silent because she dinna want to make the situation worse by Conall and Haydon going after the culprits. She did no' remember what happened.

He'd spoken with Dorathia many times and had even asked Father Samuels, the traveling priest who had come for a visit, if he had any ideas about what his sister seemed to be suffering.

No one had an answer. Many suggestions and ideas, but no'thing helpful, except give her time and she will return to normal.

Who kenned a bump on her head would restore her sense.

"To answer your question, you were not in the best of shape. Dirty, torn clothes."

"And ye ne'er found out what happened to me and who was responsible?"

He shook his head sadly. "Nay. With you refusing to speak of it, we had no idea who to find and offer him a painful death."

For the first time since the conversation had begun, Donella smiled. "I am assuming whatever happened I've blocked from my mind, but for some reason when I knocked myself out and my memory returned, 'twas only from before I was found wandering in the woods." She shook her head. "'Tis verra strange."

"I wish I could tell ye more, sister, but I am happy that ye have returned to us."

Donella offered a slight smile. "Until mayhap my memory of that incident returns and I am no longer myself. Or myself who I used to be. Or who I am now." She shook her head and grinned.

* * *

SHE LEFT Haydon's solar and carefully wandered down the stairs to the great hall. "Can I get ye something, my lady?" One of the serving lasses, a new one, most likely the daughter of another servant in the house, approached her.

Remembering she ne'er had a nooning since the fight

had broken out at the ale house, she said, "Aye. Can I have a mug of ale and whatever the cook has handy that will fill me until the evening meal."

She gazed around the room while she waited and thought of how she'd forgotten to ask Haydon about the remark the mon from the alehouse had made about thinking her family had locked her away.

Was she really so verra different? She nodded at the lass as she placed a bowl of soup, with bread and butter and a mug of ale.

Her thoughts turned to Callum. The mon in the alehouse had insulted him, as well. Said his brother threw him out of the Gunn clan because he was a coward. If she was trying to solve her own problems and answer her own questions, mayhap she could help with Callum's situation as well.

Ainslee had told her Callum had come to them requesting permission to join their clan since he'd been banned from his own by his verra own brother, the new laird. Whatever the reason was he gave him, 'twasna good enough, so being a verra suspicious mon, Haydon had denied him, and it was when Callum was leaving that she fell down the stairs and he saved her from a certain death. Whether it was through guilt or gratitude, Haydon allowed him to stay temporarily and sent a missive to the mon's brother to hear what he had to say.

Whether he'd received a reply or no', she'd ne'er heard any more about it from Ainslee. Since the Gunn clan bordered the Sutherland lands, it would no' have taken long to get a reply to Haydon's message, so apparently whatever Callum's issue was with his brother, it wasna enough to make Haydon order him to pack up and leave.

After finishing her meal, she wandered over to Dorathia's small cottage on the inside of the castle walls. The healer was there, mixing up potions for her patients.

"Can ye do with some help? I seem to be lost. I ken there is always work in the gardens, but I doona feel like pulling weeds."

"Aye, I can always use the help. I expect my niece Helena to return in the next few weeks. If yer wanting to help, I could use young, strong arms to crush the flowers so I can make healing drinks from them."

Once they began to work together, Donella said, "Do ye remember me when I was a child?"

The healer smiled and nodded. "Aye, indeed. Ye were a sweet little lass, always getting yerself into trouble. I think 'twas because as the only girl and the youngest, yer mam and da didn't do as much fussing with ye as they had with Conall and the laird."

"From what I learned today from Haydon, it might have been better for me if they had 'fussed' at me more."

Dorathia looked at her. "What did ye learn today, lass?"

Donella started plummeting the herbs with a vengeance. "No' as much as I had hoped to learn."

When Dorathia dinna say anything, Donella said, "I was led to believe I was given enough freedom that something horrible happened to me." She stopped pounding the flowers. "Did ye ken about it?"

Now Dorathia became verra busy in measuring herbs and oils. "Aye, lass, I did. I was the one who took care of ye when they found ye."

No' sure she wanted the answer, she asked the question, anyway. "All Haydon told me was that I was dirty, and my clothes were ripped."

Dorathia wiped her fingers on a clean cloth. "If yer sure ye want to hear the whole story—as I ken it—I'll tell ye, but are ye sure ye doona want to just forget it, keep it at the back of yer mind where yer brain has pushed it?"

Donella shook her head. "I am three and twenty years, Dorathia. According to just about everyone I've met, I am no' the person I used to be before I fell down the stairs and smacked my head." She took a deep breath. "I believe Haydon never arranged for a marriage for me because of that."

The words came tumbling from her mouth, like a brook after a heavy rain. "Everyone is so surprised to see me, to talk to me, like I've been asleep for years. The reason Callum got injured was because one of the men in the alehouse said he thought I was mad and that my family had locked me away years ago." She smiled softly. "Callum came to my defense." She frowned. "And now he's injured."

Dorathia put her work aside and said, "What is the last thing ye remembered after waking up from the knock on yer head?"

Donella thought for a moment. "I remembered falling down the stairs and being caught in the arms of a verra handsome and strong mon." She felt a warm flush rising from her middle to her face.

Dorathia grinned. "Callum Gunn."

Donella lowered her eyes. "Aye."

"What after that?"

"Nothing of importance. I remember having the worst headache of my life. Everyone spoke softly to me, and I assumed that was because of my head injury. It wasn't until I finally got tired of staying in bed and went downstairs and did what I thought was normal things and everyone began to watch me like they expected me to dance around with no clothes on or something strange like that."

Dorathia sat on a stool and took Donella's hands in hers. "When they found ye, after being missing for a few days, ye were a dirty mess. There was blood on yer clothes. I doona think Haydon would tell ye this, but with where the blood was, it appeared ye'd been violated."

Donella swallowed. Hard. Even though it might get worse, she had to hear the entire story. "What else?"

Dorathia sighed. "When I stripped ye down, since your mam was taken to her bed when they found ye, yer poor little body was covered in bruises."

Donella tried her best to remember what had happened to her. She shook her head. "'Tis almost as if yer telling me a verra sad story of something that happened to another lass."

The healer squeezed her hands. "Just promise me if ye do e'er remember what happened to ye, that ye go right away to one of yer family members. Yer going to need a lot of love and acceptance when, and if, that happens."

They worked for the rest of the afternoon in silence, with Donella's mind racing around, trying desperately to remember what happened to her. Then she would force it all to the back of her mind, telling herself it dinna matter.

"I have a potion here for Callum Gunn if ye care to see that he gets it." Dorathia pointed to a small container on the counter near her.

"Aye. I will be sure to see that he gets it." Feeling wearier than she had for a long time, she smiled faintly at Dorathia and picked up the container.

The woman gave her a hug. "Remember, Donella, whatever happens a lot of people love ye."

She nodded and left the cottage, clutching the small container in her hand. It was still about an hour until the evening meal, so she decided to check on Callum and deliver the potion.

Donella had been told by Haydon that she need no' attend to the patient and one of the lasses who worked in the kitchen would bring his meals to him. Why that annoyed her was questionable, but there it was. But now she'd been instructed by the healer to bring the liquid to him.

After knocking softly, she opened the door to his answer. She smiled when she saw him sitting up in the bed looking grouchy.

"What is wrong?"

"I am feeling fine. 'Tis nothing but a scratch, and I've had worse before."

Donella pulled up a chair close to the bed and held up her hand. "Well, I have this for ye from Dorathia. She said it would help ye sleep."

"Sleep! I want something to get me out of the bed." He grinned at her. "If ye want to keep me in bed, I can think of ways for ye to help me do that."

She gasped, despite his words that had caused her heart to beat faster and strange feelings like butterflies in her stomach. "Callum, 'tis improper for ye to speak to me like that."

"Ah, mayhap, but 'tis true."

It had just occurred to her that Callum's eyes were glazed and his cheeks flushed. She reached over and touched his forehead. "Ye have a fever, Callum. I fear 'twill be a tad longer in bed whether ye like it or no'."

"No fever. I'm just warm because it's so blasted hot in here."

"Nay. 'Tis not hot in here. Ye have a fever and I think the best thing for ye is to sleep and let yer body heal itself."

He huffed just as a knock sounded. The old wooden door moved open, and a young lass walked in, carrying a bowl of some sort of stew, along with bread and fresh butter. "I have yer evening meal, Callum."

Donella had to work hard to control herself when the itch to grab the food from the lass and show her to the door came over her. 'Twas silly. She and Callum were only friends. Just because he asked her to go to the village with him and then got injured defending her in the alehouse dinna mean much.

She stood and took the tray from the lass. "I'll see that *Mr. Gunn* eats his meal. You may leave now."

Her head snapped around when she heard a chuckle from Callum. "Are ye laughing at me?"

Despite shaking his head, the mirth in his eyes made her want to dump the bowl of stew over his head. Drawing on her dignity, she raised her chin and walked toward him. "Do ye care to eat yer meal before I give you the potion Dorathia sent ye?"

"Actually, lass, I doona feel like eating. Can ye put the tray o'er there on the table and I'll eat it later."

Donella put the tray down and then placed her hand on Callum's forehead. "Ye are getting warmer, Callum. I think if ye try to force yerself to eat right now it might come back up. I will get ye some fresh water and then ye can take the medicine from Dorathia."

"Aye, ye take good care of me, lass."

"If ye remember correctly, 'twas defending me that got ye into this bed with an injury ye refer to as a 'scratch.'

He reached out to take her hand. "We take care of each other, aye?"

8

*A*inslee kissed her four little ones on their heads and slipped out of the nursery. Jenny, the lass who worked as a nanny for them nodded at her as she settled into a chair in the room to stay until the little ones were asleep. Then she would sleep on the cot in the next room.

Even though it was still early evening, Ainslee climbed down the stairs and walked the length of the corridor until she reached the bedchamber she and Haydon shared. Before she left to see the little ones settled, he'd offered her an 'invitation' to join him there.

She smiled because even after six years of marriage and four bairns, he still wanted her just about every night. Dorathia had told her last year something she'd learned as a midwife. She had claimed that it had appeared to her that there were certain times in a woman's monthly cycle when she was unlikely to become with child.

Even though Haydon had scoffed at the idea, which

Ainslee kenned he didn't want to believe since that would put them on a schedule, they had tried it and so far, no new bairns had appeared.

He was already in bed when she arrived. "My goodness, my laird. Is yer age getting to ye, then?"

Haydon put aside the ledger he had been studying and held his hand out. "There is no'thing wrong with my age, wife. Get out of those blasted clothes and come here, and I'll show ye what an old mon can do."

And did it well, indeed.

Sometime later, wrapped in each other's arms, both slowly catching their breath, Haydon said, "I am concerned about Donella."

Ainslee shifted and rested her head on her propped-up hand. "It seems ye've been concerned about Donella since I arrived. What is yer new worry now?"

Haydon began to twirl her hair with his finger. "She came to me today and asked me to tell her why everyone is treating her so strangely."

"Oh."

"Aye."

"'Twas only a matter of time before she asked, Haydon. Donella is a smart woman. I kenned ever since I've known her that she had appeared simple-minded, but there were times I saw intelligence in her eyes."

"You've told me what had happened to her, as much as ye kenned. I assume ye told her as well. Did that help her to remember anything else?"

He shook his head. "Nay. No' only could she not tell me anything else, she dosna remember it at all." He began counting on his fingers. "Dinna remember getting lost.

Dinna remember what happened to her while she was missing. Dinna remember why her clothes were torn and why she was filthy."

"I'm not sure this means anything, but I saw her and Dorathia having an intense conversation in the cottage when I passed by to capture your son to keep him from running into the castle wall."

Haydon grinned like any proud da. "Since Finlay canno' walk yet, I assume ye mean Alasdair was giving ye chase?"

"Aye. And doona look so smug. He's going to get hurt one day."

"Aye. He will get hurt one day. I got hurt many times when I was a lad. 'Tis in the blood of a mon."

Ainslee rolled her eyes. "He's a lad of three summers."

Haydon gathered her hair and draped it over her naked shoulder.

"Do ye have any plans for Donella now that she seems to have recovered from whatever it was that held her trapped for years?"

"Plans?"

"Marriage. The lass is three and twenty summers. She should have been wedded years ago and already holding a bairn on her hip while another one fists her skirts."

"Nay." He held up his hand when she started to speak. "This recovery of hers is too new for me to be sure she is prepared to marry. Doona forget it was confirmed by Dorathia that she'd been violated while held prisoner. I'm no' sure if the healer told Donella while they spoke today, but any mon who takes her on as wife will have to ken what she'd been through. And with her memory of it gone, is there any mon ye ken willing to take on a wife with her history? Taking a chance that if the memory does return, she won't revert back again?"

"Aye."

Haydon frowned. "Who? The lass hasn't been without her memory for more than a couple of weeks."

Ainslee smiled. "Callum Gunn."

* * *

CALLUM WRITHED ON THE BED, his sheets damp from sweating, his soaked hair plastered to his head. Donella had just entered the bedchamber and was appalled at his condition.

She hurried to the bed and felt his head. He was so hot to the touch he felt as though he would burst into flames.

"I am not happy with how ye've been neglected, Callum," she murmured under her breath. She would need to cool him down with wet cloths and then change his bedding. The cooling down she could do with ease, but she would need a strong arm to move him around so she could replace the sheets.

Donella left the bedchamber and made her way downstairs—carefully—and headed to the kitchen. "Jonet, I need a bucket of cool water and some clean cloths."

"Aye, Donella." She stopped stirring the pot over the fire and turned to one of the young kitchen helpers. "Matthew, gather the things her ladyship needs." She turned to Donella. "Who needs them?"

"Mr. Gunn. He is recovering in the first bedchamber at the top of the stairs from a serious wound. Dorathia did a fine job of cleaning up the slice and sewing him back up, but he's developed the fever and needs to be cooled down."

"Ach, the poor mon. I heard he received that injury defending ye in the village."

No' happy that the story had apparently been spread around the castle, she merely nodded and turned to Matthew. "When ye get the things I need, can ye bring it to the bedchamber? I am going to Dorathia's cottage to see if there is something she can give me to help Mr. Gunn."

"Seems like a lot of fuss and bother for a warrior. Doona they get injured all the time?" One of the kitchen lasses murmured to the lass sitting next to her.

"I heard that, Felicity!" Jonet said, turning her back on the cooking pot once again. "'Tis none of yer business who gets help in this keep. Now ye apologize to Lady Donella for yer remark and plan to spend two hours after your normal time today washing dishes."

"Oh, nay, Jonet, Ye needn't do that," Donella said.

The cook shook her head. "No' to contradict ye, my lady, but discipline is needed in the kitchen."

Thinking she might have overstepped herself since she dinna ken that much about the kitchen, Donella left to see if Dorathia could give her something for Callum's fever.

The healer was just leaving her cottage when Donella reached her front door. "What's yer hurry, lass? Ye almost ran into me."

"'Tis sorry I am, Dorathia, but Mr. Gunn has developed the fever. I have asked the kitchen to bring up a bucket of cool water and some clean cloths. I was hoping ye might have something I could give him."

Dorathia grinned. "So very concerned ye are about the young mon, aye?"

Before she could sputter out an answer to that, Dorathia joined her arm in hers and started them walking to the keep. "I was just on my way to see Mr. Gunn." She patted the handle of the basket she carried under her arm. "There isna a lot to be done for the fever, but this will help him sleep more so he's not as uncomfortable while the fever does its work."

Donella looked at the healer. "I doona understand. How does a fever do its work?"

"It is thought that the fever, providing it dosna get too high, or last too long, actually helps the body to recover."

Donella shook her head. "That is verra strange. I always believed fever was a cursed thing. Something to work hard to get rid of."

They reached the keep steps and made their way through the heavy door to the great hall. "Aye, ye do want to try to keep the fever down if ye can. The worse kind of fever I've seen and verra few recover from is childbirth fever." Dorathia shook her head. "'Tis a bad thing, that. I've seen perfectly healthy women give birth to a perfectly healthy bairn, only to develop the fever and die."

"But not all women get it," Donella said as they made their way across the hall to the stairs.

"Nay. I've spoken to other midwives and no one seems to ken why one mam gets it, and another dosna. However, one midwife claimed the only women who developed childbed fever in her experience was when the midwife had just delivered another bairn for a different mam."

"How verra odd," Donella said. There was truly only so much they kenned about the human body. Why some recovered rapidly and some lingered for days until they died.

They entered the room, and Dorathia walked over to the window, and removed the animal skin covering it. "Fresh air will help cool the lad down and take some of the stuffiness out of the room."

The door to the bedchamber opened and the young lad Jonet had instructed to bring up the bucket of cool water and clothes walked in. "I have yer things here, Lady Donella."

"Thank ye, Matthew."

The young mon placed the bucket and cloths on the table next to the bed. Dorathia felt Callum's head. "Aye. The poor mon is burning up with fever." She turned to Donella. "'Tis best if we cool him down first, then change the linens on the bed."

"Aye, that's what I thought." Donella dipped the cloth into the cool water and began to wipe Callum's face and neck.

"This is fine, lass, but we need to remove some of his clothing to cool him off."

"Oh," Donella said. She dinna ken if Haydon would approve of her undressing the warrior. Then she realized 'twas all proper because Dorathia was with her, and they were dealing with a patient.

Dorathia pulled the light blanket off Callum and started to untie the front of his leine, revealing curly dark hair. Donella stopped wiping his forehead and a verra strange feeling came over her as she looked at Callum's chest. No' a good feeling but making her slightly nauseous.

Taking a deep breath, she returned to wiping his face and neck. Dorathia pushed the leine up to Callum's underarms. "Ye can start wiping down his chest, lass, that will help."

Donella's hand started to shake as she dipped the cloth into the water. Sweat broke out on her face and she took several deep breaths.

"Are ye all right, lass?" Dorathia asked, concern on her face.

"Aye. I'm fine." She squeezed the extra water out of the cloth. When she reached over to place the cloth on Callum's chest, she dropped the cloth and covered her face with her hands.

"Donella, lass, what's wrong?"

She looked up. "I doona ken. I feel verra sick all of a sudden."

"Mayhap 'tis better if ye let me do this and ye can help me change the linen later."

She shook her head furiously. "Nay. Something tells me I need to do this."

Dorathia continued to look at her oddly, but Donella had grown so used to people regarding her in a strange way, that she ignored it and forced herself to pick up the cloth lying on Callum's chest. She smoothed the cloth over his chest, all the time gagging.

She wasna sure what was going on but feared it might have something to do with her experience tucked into the back of her mind. Dorathia had already told her about being violated so of course she would react to seeing a mon's naked chest.

That thought dinna help her body's reaction to the

chore she was doing. She continued, even though she was still breathing so heavily that she felt as though she would pass out. Somewhere deep inside her she kenned she had always been a strong person. If this was a reaction to the horror she'd gone through, she would fight it.

She had no idea what she was like before she knocked herself out, but from how people have acted since then, it was not a place she wished to return to.

"Donella, ye are not looking very well, lass. I think ye should let me finish up cooling Mr. Gunn and ye take a break."

"Nay!"

Dorathia's eyes grew wide.

"I'm sorry. I dinna mean to holler at ye so." She looked up at the healer. "I believe I am reliving something that happened to me all those years ago."

The healer nodded. "Aye, I believe ye are correct. I think the sight of the mon's chest is doing that to ye."

Donella nodded. "Aye. I doona remember anything more, though. But I ken the sight of chest hair is making me nauseous and verra nervous."

"Yet ye want to continue?"

"Aye. I doona wish to return to where I was before I fell. I'm enjoying this life and doona want to give it up."

Dorathia nodded. "Well done, lass."

They continued to wipe Callum down, and Donella found as time went by she was less anxious. Her unease rose up again when they had one of the men in the kitchen join them to turn Callum so they could change his bedding.

Seeing that broad back, tight buttocks and muscular legs brought the nausea back again. Her breathing picked up as well, but she was determined to fight through it.

She wiped her damp forehead on the sleeve of her dress, took deep breaths and continued.

Eventually, the sheets were clean and dry and Callum was looking much better. "Are ye staying for a while, Donella?" Dorathia asked.

"Aye. I'll sit with him. They should be bringing his evening meal up, but I'm no' sure he will eat it."

"Most likely no' and I don't think food is good for his body right now. He needs to fight this fever, not use up his energy digesting food." Dorathia picked up her basket. "I will stop at the kitchen and ask Jonet to send up some medicinal tea and mayhap some meat broth." She held up the small bottle of liquid. "Ye can give him this when he awakens. Try to have him drink some of the broth and tea before ye give it to him."

"Aye," Donella said as she brushed back the locks from Callum's forehead.

'Twas verra quiet once Dorathia had left and the lass from the kitchen brought up the tea and broth, eyeing Donella nervously as she placed the tray on the table and hurried from the room.

Donella reached out and took Callum's hand. "'Tis sad that I fell apart so easily when we were trying to cool ye off. I ken ye can't hear me, but I want ye to ken that when ye awaken I will tell ye what I learned from Haydon."

With a sigh, she leaned back and eyed the trencher of food the kitchen lass had brought up for her. Since her stomach was now settled, she might try to take the bit of bread on the tray.

She was chewing slowly, studying Callum's face when

he opened his eyes. "Ach, lass. 'Twas ye who cooled me off." His voice sounded as though he'd swallowed a frog.

"Yes. Dorathia and I worked verra hard to do so." She placed the bread back on the tray. "How do ye feel?"

"No' as hot was I was feeling before. The pain in my arm is a tad troubling, but I think I am on the mend. How long have I been suffering with the fever?"

"I'm not exactly sure. I came here earlier today and ye were tossing and turning and burning up with fever. I went to Dorathia's cottage to get something for ye and she was already on her way here. Between the two of us, we got ye cooled down and the sheets changed."

"Thank ye. I shouldna' e'en be here. They should have brought me to the warrior's quarters."

"Nay. There was no way ye would have recovered over there."

Callum reached out and took her hand in his. She noticed it was dry and not as warm. "I'm glad yer here, lass, but I doona want you to get into trouble with the laird."

"Do no' trouble yerself over that. I've been here all afternoon and Ainslee stopped in once so Haydon kens I'm here."

Donella took a deep breath. "I ken that we are only friends—"

Callum squeezed her hand. "—Nay, more than friends, I hope, Donella. As soon as I am on my feet, I intend to ask yer brother if I may court ye."

She blushed, 'twas what she wanted as well. She hesitated for a moment, then took a deep breath.

"What is it, lass?

"Before ye take that step, I need to tell ye about a conversation I had earlier today with my brother."

Callum frowned. "Ye look so frightened."

"Aye. I am. 'Twas no' a happy conversation, but if ye are planning to speak with Haydon about us, then ye need to hear what he had to say, and what Dorathia also told me."

9

*C*allum and Donella were clinging to each other's hands when she finished her story. Both Haydon's information and Dorathia's.

"Ye did a fine job of telling the tale, sweetheart. I doona want to push ye for more, since I can see this has caused ye a great deal of distress."

"Aye, but every time I speak of it, the telling gets easier." She shook her head. "I'm no' sure I want to ken more of it." She sighed and looked Callum in the eye. "Are ye sure ye still wish to speak with Haydon about courting me?"

He raised his hand and cupped her cheek. "Lass, I want to court ye more than ever. Ye are a strong woman and if the horror of what ye suffered should return, I want to be the mon who helps ye through it."

A small tear slid down her cheek. He wiped it with his thumb. She felt a sense of relief at Callum's words.

"Now that ye had yer broth and tea, I have something here Dorathia gave me to help ye sleep again so yer body can heal." Donella reached behind her to the table alongside the bed.

"I will take it, Donella, but no more after this. I'm a warrior and canno' be lying about in bed like an old woman."

"All right, I will let Dorathia ken ye want no more." She reached out and touched his forehead. "Ye are getting a tad warm again."

He took the cup of liquid Donella held out to him. "Ach, lass, 'tis no'thing. In the morning I will be up and back on the lists."

Donella sat with him until he fell asleep, then made her way quietly out of the room. Ainslee was just about to enter the room when Donella left.

"How is he doing?" Ainslee asked.

"His fever is back, but the stubborn mon insists he will return to the lists in the morning."

Ainslee joined arms with Donella and moved them forward. "Ach, sister, ye might as well learn that men doona feel their worth unless they are waving their sword around."

Apparently on her way to Haydon's solar, Donella stopped them as they reached the door. "Can I ask ye something?"

"Of course. What is it ye want to ken?"

Donella sighed and looked away. "Callum plans to speak with Haydon about courting me."

She wasn't sure what she expected, but when Ainslee said nothing for a few moments, Donella looked at her with anxiety. "What is it?"

Ainslee smiled. "Ach, doona fash yerself, lass. 'Twill be no surprise to yer brother. We have both noticed the attachment ye both seemed to form almost from the time Callum caught ye in his arms as ye flew down the stairs like a bird."

"I had a conversation with Haydon and Dorathia about what happened to me all those years ago."

Ainslee nodded.

"Then I dinna want to remember what had been missing from the story." She looked at Ainslee. "Does that make me a weak woman?"

Ainslee hugged her. "Nay. Ye are a strong woman, and if the memory comes back to ye, I ken ye will overcome it now that ye have many who love ye."

"Thank ye, sister. I want more than anything to have a normal life. I doona remember how I was before the fall, but from what I've been told and how I've been treated, I will fight with all my mind and body to keep from becoming that person again."

"I have faith in ye, Donella." Ainslee opened the door to Haydon's solar and Donella continued downstairs.

* * *

After only a few hours on the List, Callum was exhausted, but refused to give up. Until Malcolm walked up to him as he was bent over, trying his best to keep from collapsing on the ground like an old woman.

"So ye think yer in good e'ough shape to defend the castle, lad?"

Callum was afraid to shake his head in denial since he kenned that was all he needed to finish his humiliation and either pass out or bring up his last meal at Malcolm's feet.

"Nay, but I canna lie around in bed like some weak lass."

"Ach, so ye think the lasses here in the keep are weak, do ye? Would ye care to spread that word, lad?"

Callum stood. "Nay."

Malcolm slapped him on the back. "Go into the great hall and have an ale. When yer finished, the laird wishes to speak with ye in his solar."

So, the time had come. He had planned to speak with Haydon as soon as he'd risen from his bed, but the laird was away from the keep for a few days dealing with an issue involving a few of his tenants near the Gunn border. Callum hoped the reason the laird wanted to see him had nothing to do with his brother.

With his arm pounding in pain, he struggled to make it to the keep. One of the lasses brought him a cool mug of ale which he downed, probably too fast, but between being verra thirsty and anxious to see the laird, he dinna have time to linger over his drink.

Feeling better after having the ale and resting his arm, he climbed the stairs and made his way to the laird's solar. A quick knock on the door was followed by "Enter."

Haydon waved to the chair in front of his large desk. He was writing in a ledger and once he finished, he laid his pen down and leaned back in his chair.

"How is the arm?"

"Getting better, Laird. I've returned to the lists."

"That's what I've heard. Ye donna think 'tis too soon?"

"Nay. Would ye continue to lay around in bed had this been yer injury?"

Haydon grinned. "Good answer, lad."

"Malcolm said ye wanted to speak with me."

"Aye. From what I've been told, ye had asked for a chance to speak with me."

Callum took a deep breath. "I wanted to request yer permission to court yer sister, Donella."

After a nerve tightening minute, Haydon nodded. "It seems to me ye only asked a few days ago to go with her to the village. What has changed so much?"

"I have a great deal of respect for yer sister and I would like to get to ken her better."

"And why should I allow that? What do ye have to offer my sister?"

"No' much in the way of coin since ye ken my brother has banned me from my clan. I work hard here, and ye have my loyalty."

"Aye. But how will that benefit Donella?"

"With yer permission, I would build us a small house outside the castle and—"

"Yer getting ahead of yerself, Gunn." He reached for a parchment on his desk. "I have an interesting missive here. It just arrived this morning."

Callum frowned. "Aye?"

"'Tis a request to negotiate a contract of marriage for Lady Donella Sutherland."

Callum fisted his hands on his lap. "How many requests for a betrothal have ye received in the past?"

Haydon dinna hesitate. "None."

"Think ye 'tis odd ye received one now that Donella has recovered from her prior issues?"

The door to the solar opened and Conall entered. "Ye wished to speak with me, Haydon?"

The laird waved to the other chair next to Callum. "Aye. 'Tis something here that we need to discuss.

Although the final decision is mine, I would care for yer opinion."

Callum was confused. If he wanted to talk to him about his request to court Donella, why would he do it here, in front of Conall? Then a thought struck him. Conall said the laird had sent for him. If what he wanted to go over with his brother was Callum's request, how did he ken he would ask such? 'Twas verra strange.

Haydon picked up the piece of parchment again. "I received this a few hours ago. 'Tis a request for Donella's hand in marriage."

Conall continued to study his brother. "And who is the request coming from?"

Haydon looked over at Callum. "Laird Fraser Gunn."

Callum jumped up from his seat, his hands fisted at his sides. "My brother? Nay!"

There was silence for almost a full minute after his outburst while Haydon studied him. Callum took his seat again, his jaw so tight he thought his teeth would crumble. "I am sorry for my fit of temper, Laird. 'Twas disrespectful."

Haydon nodded.

Callum took a few breaths to calm down. He had no idea what was in his Fraser's mind, but it couldna have been good. "Since ye made sure I was here when ye revealed this request to yer brother, I assume ye kenned ahead of time that I would ask for permission to court Donella with the purpose of marriage."

"Ye ne'er mentioned marriage, but I did assume that was yer intention." Haydon leaned his forearms on the desk and looked directly at Callum. "Why do ye suppose yer brother is suddenly interested in Donella?"

"If it was anyone except my brother I would say as the new laird, it would be wise for him to form alliances, and we all ken the best way to do that is through marriage. And we all ken the Sutherland Clan is one of the best."

Conall leaned forward. "Why do ye say if it was anyone except yer brother?"

"The warrior who insulted Donella and then injured my arm was one of the Gunn clan warriors. Since yer sister and I were there together, I ken his request is another way to punish me."

"For something ye say ye dinna do," Haydon said.

"Aye. The men who claimed I fumbled on the battlefield and caused my da's death were lying. 'Tis hard to say who is near and who is far from ye when yer in the midst of a battle, but I ken my da was nowhere near me."

"Why do ye suppose yer brother wanted to ban ye, since as firstborn, he was the one who would inherit the lairdship anyway?" Conall asked.

Callum ran his fingers through his hair. "I doona ken."

Conall looked at Haydon and nodded at the piece of parchment on the desk. "What do ye plan to do about that?"

"Well, since Callum has requested permission to court our sister, I am assuming he has marriage on his mind also. She has become verra popular of late."

Conall and Haydon both looked at Callum.

He could feel the heat rise to his face like some giggling lass. "I like the lass. Verra much. She has told me as much as she kens about what happened to her—"

"—She told ye?" Haydon asked.

"Aye. I wanted her to ken that I was going to ask

permission to court her, and she felt that I needed to ken about that before I approached ye."

"Apparently it made no difference in yer intentions."

"Nay. As I said, I care a great deal for Donella, and had I more to my name, I would ask right now for her hand. But we all ken that right now all I have is my sword."

"And a good one at that," Conall added.

"Aye, but that isna enough to offer for the lass," Callum said dejectedly.

Conall looked over at Haydon. "Donella has a dowry, I assume?"

"Aye. For the last several years I never expected to use it." He glanced at Callum. "I will make my decision within a few days about yer brother's request and yers. In the meantime, based on what my wife has told me about Donella's wishes in this, I will permit ye to court her."

Callum let out a deep breath. "Thank ye, Laird."

He went to stand and Haydon said, "From what Malcolm has told me, yer pushing yerself too hard and 'twill take longer for ye to heal if ye donna give yerself a break. I suggest ye take over training the new lads who have just started working with their swords."

Callum nodded, more than pleased at the outcome of the meeting. Still concerned about his brother's request, he felt as though he had the upper hand.

As he made his way through the great hall, Donella walked up to him. "Did ye meet with my brother?"

"Aye." He took her hand. "He has given me permission to court ye."

Donella's smile would light up the entire room. "That is wonderful news."

He decided 'twas not his place to tell her about the

betrothal Haydon had received. That was up to her brother. "He also assigned me to work with the newer lads until my arm heals."

"Thank goodness." She reached up on her toes and kissed him on the lips, then flushed a bright red.

Startled, he just looked at her, then smiled. "When I kiss ye properly, sweetheart, it won't be where everyone can see us."

* * *

"What do ye make of this?" Conall pointed to the betrothal request sitting on Haydon's desk.

"I have no idea. I've never met the Gunn, and ken no'thing about him. After having Callum here for the last few weeks, I doona believe he would fumble in battle. Ye and Malcolm have had yer best men go at him in training and he is not a mon who fumbles. The question is, why would his brother have men lie to make it look so, and then ban his only brother from the clan. 'Tis a huge step to take for any clan member, especially yer own brother."

Conall nodded. "I agree. There is more to this. What will ye do about the mon's request?"

"Since I've given Callum permission to court Donella, I would no' feel comfortable if I dinna find out more about the mon."

"Callum or The Gunn?"

"The Gunn. I've seen enough of Callum to trust him. And for the first time in many years, our sister is not only comfortable with a mon, but seems to not object to being courted."

"Have ye told her what ye ken about what happened to her all those years ago?"

"Aye. I told her as much as I kenned, which you ken isna much. Apparently, after speaking with me, Donella went to Dorathia, and she gave her more information. Things that I would not be comfortable sharing with her."

Conall nodded his agreement.

"According to the healer, none of what she told her brought back any memories."

"What sort of dowry does Donella have?" Conall asked, changing the conversation.

"Some coin, and a little bit of land. I think if this courtship works out for her and Callum, 'twould be better to let him use the funds to build them a house. He doesna appear to be the type who would be comfortable living off his wife's family."

"The land you granted to Malcolm and his labor here has worked out quite well for him and Christine."

"Aye." Haydon tapped on the parchment sitting on his desk. "I'll hold off answering this for a while. See how things progress."

"'Tis a fine thing to see our sister happy for the first time in years."

"Indeed. During that dark time, I would have given anything to see Donella return to the way she used to be before her disappearance. If this mon can make her happy, then I owe him a great deal. No' only did he save her life, but he also saved her life in another way."

"Aye," Conall said. "However, I do worry about how Callum would handle her if those memories all come back."

"If the mon cares for her the way he said, I doona

think it would be a problem. He's a strong mon and deep inside Donella, she is strong as well."

"All of this talk raises questions in me again about what happened to her. Who did it, and why he was never found. We scoured the area for weeks after we found Donella." Conall stood, ready to leave. "'Tis my guess it was someone passing through and seeing her alone in the woods grabbed her and kept her with him. What we ne'er learned was how long she was in his hands and how long she wandered around after she escaped. Or, did she escape? We e'er learned anything from the lass.."

* * *

"Care to go for a walk, Lady Donella?" Callum reached his hand out.

They had just finished the evening meal and Callum had taken the time to clean himself up and change his clothes before he'd entered the great hall to eat.

The other warriors at the tables where they ate were busy getting great laughs at his expense, trying their best to embarrass him, but he had too great a prize to work hard for to let that bother him.

"Yes, Mr. Gunn, I would like that." Donella took his hand and he helped her down from the dais.

"Is it permissible to walk with Lady Donella outside the keep, but within the castle walls?" Callum asked Haydon as he took Donella's arm and linked it with his.

"Aye." The laird's grin encouraged more comments and laughter from the other warriors.

Once they were outside, Donella said, "I doona understand why there is such attention put onto us. Ye would think no one had ever courted before."

Callum patted her hand as it rested on his arm. "Doona fash yerself, sweetheart. I think they're just jealous because I'm walking with the most beautiful woman in the castle."

Donella flushed.

It was a warm evening for the Highlands, even for early August. The mixture of the summer air mixed with Donella's own unique scent was driving him crazy.

The sky was lit up with millions of stars, a brilliant sight, but no' better than the beautiful lass at his side. He walked them far enough from the keep and the warriors on the castle parapet from seeing them. Once he felt they had enough cover, he leaned against the stone wall and pulled her against him. "Ach, lass. I've been wanting to do this for days." He reached up and smoothed the hair from her forehead. "Yer so beautiful, it takes my breath away."

"If ye keep this up, Mr. Gunn, ye'll have me staring at my looking glass all day." She grinned and placed her hands on his chest.

"I want to thank ye for taking care of me while I was injured."

"'Twas what I wanted to do." She rubbed her thumbs over his neck which was slowly driving him crazy. If he dinna stop her soon, he would take her up against the wall. Which would kill any chance he had with her brother to accept his proposal.

"I feel like I'm getting better," she whispered. "Only a few weeks ago, I could never imagine standing here with ye, alone in the dark."

"I'll ne'er do anything to frighten ye, Donella. Ye must

ken that. If e'er ye feel uncomfortable, just let me ken." He cupped her cheeks in his hand. "I want ye for more than what we can do in bed." He grinned. "Although that is important, too, but I want ye forever."

Donella sucked in a breath. "What are ye saying?"

"That I want to marry ye, Donella. We came close to discussing that in my meeting with Conall and the laird today. They ken my intentions. Now I want ye to ken them."

He held his breath as Donella studied his face. "I think 'tis a good idea, Callum." She moved her hands up to his shoulders. "I have strong feelings for ye, and I think if anyone can help me to face whatever I need to if my memory returns, 'tis ye."

"Ach, lass." He lowered his mouth and covered hers, nipping at her lips until she opened for him.

Just as he entered her mouth, she drew back. "Nay." She shook her head. "Nay."

He closed his eyes, forcing himself to be patient.

10

Despite the problems with their last visit to the village, Callum and Donella set out once more on a cool Thursday afternoon, the day the crofters and other vendors from the surrounding area came to the Sutherland Village.

This time Donella was happy to note that very few people seemed surprised to see her. The discomfort of the last trip melted away as vendors greeted her, smiled, and offered to show her the various items they had on display.

"Do ye care for a new ribbon, Donella?" Callum asked as he pulled her toward a table with various items, including wool scarves, necklaces, and colorful grosgrain ribbons.

"Aye, I would always want a new ribbon."

They took their time looking over the table; Callum purchased a ribbon and promised the vendor to buy a scarf from him when the weather grew cold once again.

"I'm feeling a tad hungry. Do ye want to try the alehouse again, or mayhap one of the meat pies that smell so good from that table over there?" Callum nodded in the direction of a mon passing out wonderful smelling meat pies as fast as the woman with him could put them into his hands.

"Ach, Lady Donella. 'Tis good to see ye again, lass. And who is this fine mon with ye?" Boris Sutherland and his wife, Ellen had been selling meat pies in the village from when Donella was a young girl. She hadn't seen them for years, but then again that was most likely because she'd been in hiding, her family had told her.

"'Tis good to see ye and yer wife as well, Boris." She turned to Callum. "Mr. Callum Gunn is one of our warriors."

Boris's eyebrows rose. "Gunn, aye?"

"Yes, sir," Callum said. "Our laird has accepted me into the clan and I now train the young warriors."

Boris slapped Callum on the back. "'Tis a fine thing to have a welcome from our laird."

Callum purchased two meat pies for them, and they ate them and drank mugs of ale from the table set up in front of the alehouse. Donella was enjoying the afternoon and dinna want it to end. She and Callum held hands during their venture and a few villagers who had seen her the last time, commented on how happy she looked and the handsome mon at her side.

Eventually, the air grew cooler, and the vendors began packing up their goods. Callum glanced at the sky. "I think we're in for some rain, 'tis a good time to leave."

She looked up and nodded her agreement.

Callum took the ribbon from her hand and tucked it into the sporran that hung at his side. Clasping her hand, he tugged Donella and they began their hurried return to the castle.

The great hall had begun to fill up with the warriors and other clan members who ate at the castle each evening. Before they separated for her to join her family Callum had the inclination to lean forward and kiss Donella right there in the great hall and longed for the day when he could do that without causing an uproar from her brothers.

"Would ye care for a game of chess after supper?" Callum asked.

"Aye. I would like that. I must warn ye, however that I am a verra good player."

Callum winked at her. "Then we shall see if ye can beat me, since I am a verra good player, as well." With a squeeze of her hand, he walked toward the warrior's table and Donella headed to her family.

* * *

THE NEXT AFTERNOON, Donella entered Haydon's solar. "Ye wished to speak with me, brother?"

When she noticed Conall was there, both of them looking quite serious, she said, "Is something amiss?"

"Nay, Donella," Haydon said. "Doona fash yerself. 'Tis something we want to discuss with ye."

She sat next to Conall and placed her hands in her lap.

Haydon leaned his forearms on his desk. "I'm sure Callum told ye that he asked my permission to court ye."

"Aye."

"How do ye feel about the lad?"

She could feel the blood rush to her face and began to shift in her chair. "I like Callum. Verra much."

Conall turned and looked at her. "He told us his intention is to ask for yer hand in marriage."

Donella nodded.

"There is no other way to ask this, and 'tis no' my intention to upset or embarrass ye, sister, but do ye think ye can handle the attentions of a husband?" Now Conall's face was the one with a red flush. 'Twas obviously not a comfortable question, but she understood why her brothers would feel the need to ask. They were only looking out for her interests.

She hesitated slightly since 'twas a question she had thought of herself many times since she'd kenned Callum. "I donna ken for sure, to be honest. As much as I hate speaking of this with ye, I understand yer concern. But I want what ye both have. Happiness and bairns. I'm intelligent enough to ken I canno' have those things if I doona marry."

Haydon and Conall looked at each other and then Haydon picked up a piece of parchment from his desk. "I have a missive here from a neighboring laird requesting we enter into negotiations with him for a betrothal."

Donella's eyes grew wide, and she jerked her head up. "For me?"

"Aye."

She let out a breath and leaned back in her chair. "I doona understand. Have there been other offers before now that I was unaware of?"

Haydon shook his head.

Her mind was in a whirl. Why would there suddenly

be a request for her hand in marriage? When neither of her brothers said a word, she asked, "Who is the laird?"

"Laird Gunn."

Donella jumped up from her seat with such force, it almost tipped over. "Gunn? Ye mean the man who banned his only brother from the clan for false accusations? That Gunn?"

"Calm yerself sister," Conall said, touching her arm.

She continued to stare at Haydon. "I ken as my laird ye have the right to make this decision, but I hope ye are no' seriously considering it."

"I wouldn't force ye to marry anyone, Donella. I am just interested to ken why this came from the mon now."

She frowned and took her seat. "The mon who insulted me in the alehouse was one of the Gunns. He must have reported the clash to his laird and he decided it wasn't enough to ban his brother, he had to also make an offer for the woman he was most likely courting."

Haydon linked his fingers together and tapped his lips with his index fingers. "The reason I presented this to ye is because a match with a laird is much more advantageous than one with a warrior."

She was up from her seat again. "An *honorable* warrior! One who received a nasty injury while defending me. A mon who ye trust enough to court me, and to swing a sword as a warrior in yer clan."

Conall sighed again. "Be at ease, Donella. No one is saying anything against Callum. If ye feel ye are ready for marriage, it would be remiss of our laird no' to tell ye of a beneficial offer."

Before he even finished his sentence, Donella snorted and was shaking her head. She took her seat again and realized that if she had a chance to enjoy a normal life with a husband and bairns, he would have to be Callum.

Did she love him?

Probably.

Did he love her?

She grinned. Probably.

Her thoughts finished, she stood. "If ye doona plan to pursue this any further, I shall leave and visit with Dorathia and see if I can offer some help."

* * *

ONCE THE DOOR CLOSED, Haydon said, "I'd like to send word to The Gunn that we are no' interested in negotiating for Donella's hand, but I'd like to find out more information about the mon first."

"Like why he made false accusations against his brother and then banned him from the clan?" Conall asked. "'Tis not an honorable thing to do."

"Aye." Haydon fiddled with the parchment on his desk. "I dinna think Donella would be amenable to this offer but I wanted to hear what she had to say. It appears her loyalty to Callum is strong."

"Mayhap it's time to put Callum at ease and tell him ye have no objection to a match between him and Donella." Conall linked his fingers over his middle and grinned.

Just then the door to the solar opened and Ainslee entered, dragging Alasdair behind her. The lad had what appeared to be flour all over his wee body.

"I want ye to see what yer son did when Jonet left the kitchen for only a few minutes to gather some items from the larder."

Haydon burst out laughing. Based on Ainslee's frown, 'twas not the response his wife had wanted. He reached out and pulled the lad close to him, even though his front was now covered with flour himself. "What were ye doing, lad?"

"Baking a cake."

"Yer a tad young to be baking cakes." He looked up at Ainslee. "Where is Jenny?"

"The lass came down with a fever, so I've been trying to keep track of all four of yer bairns."

"Ach. Why is it when they're in trouble, they become *my* bairns?"

"For the verra same reason that ye laughed like a fool when I dragged Alasdair in here. If ye think this is so amusin' mayhap I should bring the four of them in here so they can entertain ye."

Haydon's grin faded and he held up his hand. "Nay."

Despite his messy state, he pulled his son onto his lap. "Ye ken yer no' supposed to go into the kitchen, aye? 'Tis a dangerous place for a lad and ye could seriously hurt yerself."

Alasdair pushed his thumb into his mouth and bent his head. "Aye."

Haydon lifted the lad's chin with his finger. "Then stay up in the nursery where ye canna get into trouble." Haydon looked at Ainslee. "See if ye can get one of the maids to help ye out."

She nodded and sighed. "Come here, Alasdair. Ye need to be cleaned up and 'tis growing close to yer nap time."

"Before ye leave, wife, I want ye to ken that ye will be making wedding plans verra soon."

She lifted the messy child into her arms. "Donella?"

"Aye. I'm giving permission to Callum to ask for her hand. I have no reason to believe she will turn him down."

"What about the offer from The Gunn?"

"I ne'er considered it but was interested to see how Callum and Donella felt about it."

Ainslee raised her eyebrows. "And?"

"They both emphatically—without being disrespectful to their laird—reacted negatively to it."

His wife smiled. "Aye, 'tis high time we had a wedding. As soon as Donella tells me she is betrothed, I shall get with Jonet and plan the wedding feast."

Haydon laughed. "Give the lad time to offer his proposal and Donella to accept it."

"Ach. *He* will and *she* will." With those words, she left the room, mumbling to Alasdair who only smiled at her.

* * *

THE GREAT HALL was filled with clanfolk, loud, boisterous warriors and the Sutherland family. Empty platters and trenchers covered the tables. With a bit of nervousness, Callum stood and walked to where the Sutherlands were all seated.

He reached his hand out toward Donella. "Care to take a stroll, lass?"

She nodded and stood, taking his hand. They seemed to gain the notice of her family and others in the great hall as they walked toward the door. They stepped into the inner bailey. "'Tis a beautiful night."

"Aye, I agree, lass, but the beautiful part of the night is ye."

"There ye go again. I donna think I am beautiful."

He moved them so they were again out of view of the warriors on duty and anyone leaving the great hall. He turned her towards him and cupped her cheeks. "Aye, ye are beautiful, but I won't argue the point with ye. I'd rather do this." He lowered his head and his lips joined hers. Her lips were sweet, warm, and plump.

So as not to upset her like the last time, he kept his tongue in his mouth and just enjoyed the feel of her sweetness. He pulled back and rested his forehead on hers. "Ach, love, yer lips drive me crazy."

She looked up at him, and he noted no fear in her eyes. He leaned in again and kissed her forehead, her cheeks, and when she dinna push him away, his lips wandered down farther and sucked on her ear. He felt a slight stiffening of her body, but then she relaxed.

"That's it, *mo ghraidh*. Relax."

Callum pulled her closer, so their bodies met. Donella slowly moved her hands up his chest and then encircled his neck. Callum made his way down to her jaw and continued his light kisses.

When his hand moved to her bottom to pull her closer, she pushed him away. "That is enough for now."

He held in his groan. 'Twas going to be a painful journey to eventually get Donella in bed, but she was worth the effort. Now 'twas probably the best time to speak to her about their future.

He grasped her hands in his and stared into her crystal blue eyes. "I have been granted permission from the laird to offer ye marriage." He pulled her hands up to his lips and kissed the backs. "I want verra much to be yer husband. To be the mon who protects ye and cares for ye.

The mon who gives ye bairns." She flinched at his last comment. "What say ye?"

Donella closed her eyes. "I care verra much for ye, Callum. I canno' imagine any other mon as my husband." She opened her eyes, tears brimming on the edges. "Ye ken what happened to me. And ye do no' ken what also happened because I can't remember myself, except that Dorathia told me I had been…violated." She barely got the word out.

He pulled her against his body, offering comfort and protection.

"If we marry, I canno' promise I will be at ease with the marriage bed."

Callum placed his hands on her shoulders. "I am aware of that. I will go slow, and not push you beyond what yer comfortable with."

"But ye will want bairns. So do I. Suppose I never get over this?"

He kissed her knuckles again. "I believe ye will get over it. Remember we are both young, we will be married many years."

She shook her head. "Ye are so trustful, Callum."

"I will just ask ye one thing, lass."

"What is that?"

"Let me try. No' now, but once we're married. Let me try to help ye overcome what has been torturing ye for years. I ken ye can do it because yer a strong woman. Just give it time and promise me ye will let me try."

Donella slowly nodded. "Aye. I accept yer proposal, Callum." She grinned and the happiness in her face strengthened his confidence that together they could overcome this.

He took her hand. "Shall we go talk to the laird? I need to make arrangements with him and I'm guessing ye will need to see Ainslee about planning the wedding."

They headed back to the keep where the great hall was cleared of the results from supper, the tables having been pushed back to the walls while three men played music. Some of the clanfolk were dancing, others were sitting and clapping and tapping their feet.

Haydon, Ainslee, Conall and Maura were among those clapping in time to the music.

Callum and Donella walked up to them. "Laird, when ye have time, I would like to speak with ye," Callum said.

Ainslee and Maura looked at each other and smiled.

"Since I ken why ye want to speak with me, let's say ye come to my solar first thing in the morning. Right now I want to spend some time dancing with my beautiful wife." Haydon took Ainslee's hand in his and led her to the area where the folk were dancing.

"What say ye, Maura? Are ye up for a dance, as well?"

"Aye, husband. I would like that," she said.

Once the two couples walked off, Callum said, "How about ye, lass? Would ye care for a dance, too?"

Donella viewed the dancers and turned to Callum. "I donna believe I ken how to dance. Can ye show me?"

He leaned down, close to her ear. "I will show ye anything ye want, lass. Just give me time."

* * *

DONELLA HAD no idea a wedding could be arranged so quickly. 'Twas only two weeks since Callum had proposed to her and here she was preparing to meet him at the kirk in the outer bailey.

They had been in luck because Father McNeil had been visiting at the MacKay clan for a wedding there, and being so close they were able to arrange their marriage ceremony quickly.

"Donella, ye look beautiful," Ainslee said as she and Maura viewed the bride after putting the ring of small flowers in her hair.

They had sewn a lovely pale blue light wool gown with lace around the bodice and at the end of the long sleeves. It fit her perfectly and made her feel like a bride. She giggled. That, of course was what she was.

She smiled softly at her two sisters-by-marriage. "'Tis quite certain ye had ne'er expected to see me as a bride."

Maura kissed her on the cheek. "Times change, and we change as well. I am sure this will be a happy marriage for ye. 'Tis apparent to everyone that Callum cares a great deal for ye, and I can see the love in yer eyes when ye look at him."

Love? She smiled. Aye, she loved Callum Gunn. For so many reasons she couldna count, starting with landing in his arms as she tumbled down the stairs.

"'Tis ready I am," she said as she took one final glance in the looking glass and headed for the door.

11

Callum nervously awaited Donella to appear at the door of the kirk situated in the corner of the outer bailey. Had the lass changed her mind? Did she decide she could ne'er perform the duties of a wife, after all?

"Ye can stop worrying, Callum," Conall said. "My sister dinna change her mind. Even the years she was lost to us, she ne'er changed her mind about anything. That habit of hers drove Haydon crazy many a time."

Conall was acting as his witness and Callum was grateful since it provided proof that the two brothers trusted him with their beloved sister. His soon-to-be brother-by-marriage provided proof for anyone in the clan who questioned he, an outsider, had the right to marry the laird's sister.

Ainslee walked up to the kirk and smiled at Callum. "Be at ease, Donella is on her way with Haydon."

He pretended that he wasna worried, but dinna fool Conall who laughed. 'Twould no' be the best thing to do on yer wedding day to punch the bride's brother in the nose.

Within minutes, Callum lost his breath when Haydon appeared from across the courtyard to the kirk. The lass on his arm was not only beautiful, but her smile lit up her face which told him she had no' decided marriage was no' for her.

Haydon handed her over to Callum and kissed his sister on the cheek.

Donella gripped his arm as they turned to the priest. He could feel her shaking and leaned down close to her ear. "'Twill be fine, *mo ghraidh*. Just take a deep breath and ye will feel better."

She offered him a shaky smile. "If I take another deep breath I will swoon."

He so wished he could take her into his arms and comfort her. 'Twas a big step for any woman to pledge the rest of her life to a mon, but given Donella's past, 'twas a huge step for her. He understood her anxiety and wanted to spend the rest of his life taking care of her and making sure nothing bad ever happened to her again.

So busy ruminating, before he kenned it, the priest requested they put the palms of their hands together before he wrapped them in a piece of Sutherland tartan.

Since Haydon had accepted him as one of their clan, he wore the traditional Sutherland formal clothing for the wedding. He did feel strange not wearing the formal Gunn tartan, but Laird Gunn had banished him, and shortly after he'd arrived at Dornoch Castle, he'd knelt before Haydon and pledged his loyalty, so he was a Gunn clan member no more.

A touch of sadness swept over him. He was marrying

the woman of his choice with none of his family members, or even clan members, present to witness the event. 'Twas then that it hit him that he had truly been banned from his clan.

Before he kenned it, their hands were unwrapped and they were officially married. He leaned forward and kissed Donella briefly on the lips. They turned to face the crowd that had gathered and smiled at each other as they cheered.

"'Tis time to celebrate," Malcolm shouted and waved his arm in the air. He was greeted with resounding cheers.

The wedding guests made their way to the great hall.

* * *

DONELLA WAS verra happy with how Ainslee, Maura and Christine, Malcolm's wife, had decorated the great hall. It seemed like flowers were everywhere, on the tables, among the rushes which set off a pleasant smell as one walked on them, and outlining the huge fireplace which was possible since it was summer.

"The ladies did a fine job," Callum said as he led her to the dais where the rest of her family sat. Serving lasses came from the kitchen, carrying platters of meat, vegetables and warm bread.

He placed his hand over hers. "Are ye feeling better, lass?"

"Aye. I think most brides have a moment of panic."

"'Tis true. I've seen many marriages at the Gunn keep. Even one lass fainted before the priest was able to wrap their hands together."

"Men doona seem to understand that women give up

so much when they marry. They are no longer free to make their own decisions or go where they want to without permission."

"Ach, lass. No' much has changed for ye, only now instead of yer brother making the decisions that affect ye and granting ye permission to go places, 'tis me now."

She couldn't help but wonder how things might have turned out if Haydon had refused to let her wander about so much. 'Twas surely the reason why she had fallen into evil hands and suffered what she couldn't remember.

At the time, Haydon had just taken over the lairdship, and being quite young, was handling so much already. One thing for certe, she wouldna e'er allow a lass of hers to leave the castle walls. But then, with as protective as Callum was, it was not likely to become a problem. She would be fortunate if she was allowed anywhere without a guard.

"I doona what has ye frowning, wife, but ne'er worry again about being hurt or harmed in any way. I shall protect ye with my life."

She watched her new husband as he spoke and couldn't help but stare at that verra handsome face. His full lips, deep green eyes, and the ever-present strands of hair that fell out of the leather string that held his hair back, had her heart taking a few extra beats.

Then her mind wandered to what would happen when the celebration ended. She kenned what was expected of her, but she also kenned that her husband would ne'er force her.

Once again he claimed her thoughts. "I have no idea why yer mind keeps wandering, lass, but I suggest ye eat some of this wonderful food."

She and Callum shared a trencher, and he'd filled theirs with the best selections. "Aye, ye have the right of it. Jonet has outdone herself this time."

Once the food had been consumed, the tables were cleared off and pushed back against the wall. She and Callum were expected to hold hands and circle the room, with her family following, and then other clan folk to introduce the dancing.

The hours that followed seemed to fly by. She and Callum spent a great deal of time dancing. Even though she wasna sure of most of the steps, he guided her, always smiling at her attempts to follow him.

She flew from partner to partner. Both of her brothers and her cousin Malcolm took her to the floor and tried to pretend she kenned what she was doing.

But it was only in Callum's arms where she felt comfortable. Safe even. Just when she felt as though she was about to collapse, he leaned down and spoke into her ear. "'Tis time to leave, *mo ghraidh*."

"Already?" She kenned she sounded like a bairn no' wanting to leave the party.

"Aye. I see the men eyeing me and I have a feeling they're planning the bedding ceremony."

With no memory of other weddings, she frowned. "What is that?"

"If ye let me lead ye out of the room now and upstairs to yer bedchamber, I will explain it, but trust me when I say ye doona want to get involved in one."

Since she dinna remember her two brothers' weddings, she had no idea what a bedding ceremony was, but she trusted her husband enough to ken he would do what was best.

Before she could give it more thought, he took her hand and hurried her from the room.

"Wait, Gunn, we're getting ready to do the bedding ceremony." One of the warriors, drunk from the whisky that they served at the wedding called out to Callum.

Without forewarning, Callum picked her up and raced to the stairs, taking them two at a time with the pounding of feet and shouts behind them. He hurried to her bedchamber, kicked the door open and slammed it shut with his foot.

He put her down and laughing, placed the bar across the door so no one could come in. He leaned against the door trying to catch his breath. Pulling her against his body, he said, "We made it, *mo chridhe*."

She had no idea why she was laughing, but the entire incident was quite strange. "Will ye tell me now what the bedding ceremony is?"

Callum moved them toward the bed where they sat. He put his arm around her shoulders, trying to speak over the pounding at the door by drunken guests.

"'Tis a custom for women at a wedding to bring the bride upstairs, strip her of all her clothing and place her in bed."

Her eyes grew wide. "All her clothes? Everything?"

He nodded.

"And then what?"

"Then the men come in and strip the groom, whip back the coverlet and shove him into the bed."

She felt the blood leave her face. "If they're whipping the coverlet back then 'tis possible for the men to see the naked bride."

He grinned. "Aye. Which is why I dinna want a bedding ceremony."

She flushed at his words. "That is terrible."

"Yer lucky we are no' members of the royal family. If that were the case, some of the men and women, and even the priest, would remain in the bedchamber to acknowledge that the marriage had been consummated."

She grew pale. "Ye mean…"

He fingered one of her curls. "Aye."

"Ach. That's even worse."

"From what I heard from yer brothers they both managed to dodge the bedding ceremony because neither of their wives wanted it either."

"That was verra nice of them."

"I ken. I must admit I've been part of a bedding ceremony for other men and it was great fun, but I had no intention of allowing a group of drunken warriors to get a glimpse of my naked wife."

She wrapped her arms around herself and looked over at him. "Thank ye, husband."

He placed his hands on her shoulders. "I told ye I would protect ye, and I meant from everything that would upset ye. Anything that I am able to." He leaned down and kissed her. "However, this I can do."

His kiss was as she remembered. Not threatening, but soft and tender. She couldn't help but wonder what would come next.

She'd asked Ainslee what she should expect on her wedding night, but strangely, her sister-by-marriage told her in her case *'twas best if she let her husband lead her.*

Suddenly, she realized she and her new husband were alone in her bedchamber. It appeared from the lack of noise outside the room that the men had given up and returned to the celebration downstairs.

"What do we do now?" she asked.

Callum groaned, but smiled and took her hands in his. "I suggest yer change out of yer pretty gown and put something more comfortable on."

She began to chew on her lips. "Where can I change?"

"This is a nice sized room. I suggest ye change by the bed here, and I'll wander over to one of the chairs in front of the fireplace."

She hesitated for a moment. This was now becoming real. She was in her bedchamber with a mon who was her husband. He wanted, aye probably needed, and by church law had the right, to do things to her she wasna sure she could allow.

Donella seemed frozen to the spot and her eyes began to fill with tears.

Callum studied her and pulled her back into his arms. "Lass, if ye want to sleep in yer gown, 'tis fine, too."

She shook her head, swiping vigorously at the tears on her cheeks. "Nay. I am a strong woman and I promised ye—and myself—that I would enter this marriage with the idea of having a normal life. 'Tis best to start the way we plan to go on."

He grinned and pulled her closer. "I love ye, Donella."

"And I love ye, Callum."

* * *

Despite her burst of confidence, Callum kenned he still had to go slow. "Turn around and I'll unfasten yer gown. Then ye can change right here and I'll meet ye at the fireplace. It looks like someone sent up some wine for us."

She pushed her beautiful golden red curls over her shoulder, leaving the lovely silky skin and the back of her gown exposed. With shaky hands, he undid the fasteners and then hopped up, almost knocking her off her feet. "I shall open the wine for us. Join me when yer ready."

He hurried away, breaking into a sweat. Donella felt this was nerve wracking for her, but 'twas turning into a contest of who was more shaken. 'Twas then he decided to forego any attempt this evening to bed his lovely wife. He'd give her time to get used to sleeping alongside him before he tried anything else.

It dinna take long for Donella to join him. He patted his knee. "Come sit here, lass. Yer too far away over there."

She smiled and joined him. He handed her a cup of wine, which she immediately downed.

He took the cup out of her hand. "Ach, be careful, lass. Ye donna want to be sick tomorrow."

She swung her feet back and forth and she looked like a bairn. Except his wife was no bairn. She apparently had removed all her clothing under her nightgown. Whether from the chill in the room or her body's reaction to their closeness, her nipples stood out against the thin material.

He gulped the cup of wine and took a deep breath. At this point 'twas probably best to get them both into bed. Maybe some cuddling would help, but sitting here, with her lovely breasts a few inches from his mouth gave torture a new meaning.

"What say ye we get into bed. 'Tis been a long day and I'm sure yer tired."

She almost looked disappointed. "Aye. I am a tad tired." She stood and headed to the bed.

His next dilemma was the fact that he always slept in the nude. He hadn't worn anything to bed since he'd been a lad. Well, she was the one who said they should start off the way they planned to go on. While he dinna think she meant to jump right into love making, he would still sleep in his usual manner.

By the time he arrived at the bed, she was under the bed covering, with her back to him. He touched her shoulder. "Lass, I'd like to at least kiss ye before ye go to sleep."

To his surprise, she turned back and smiled at him. She wrapped her arms around his waist. "Ye have no clothes on, husband!" She began to edge away, but he pulled her back.

"Aye. Verra observant, wife. I ne'er sleep with clothes on. Ye will get used to it." He brushed her soft, silky hair off her face and bent to kiss her. She was more enthusiastic than he'd expected.

Taking a chance, he ran his tongue against her lips and this time she dinna pull away, but dinna open her mouth, either. He began to kiss her cheeks, nose, forehead, jaw and neck. She stiffened at first, but then relaxed and sighed softly.

His hand wandered over her waist and moved up and down her back and lower to her bottom. He squeezed the firm flesh and shifted his mouth to nibble on her lips, but she still dinna allow him to enter her mouth. But he really felt as though they were making much more progress than he'd expected.

After a few more minutes of him touching her and her

stiffening, then relaxing, she pulled back, her breath coming in gasps. Slowly, she pulled up the bedclothes so his chest was covered. "I think I'm feeling weary and need some sleep."

"One more kiss?"

She hesitated for a moment. "Aye."

He pulled her against him again and made this last kiss a verra good one. He finally edged her mouth open, but after a few seconds she pulled back and wiped her mouth.

"Good night, love," he said.

"Good night, husband," she replied.

CALLUM AWOKE to screams piercing the air. He rolled over and Donella was thrashing around the bed. She kept screaming, "Nay, nay, nay. Get off, yer hurting me."

He took hold of her arms and shook her slightly. "Donella, love, yer dreaming, wake up."

She shook her head back and forth, her screams turning to moans. When he attempted to pull her into his arms, she shoved him back with her palms on his chest, taking him off guard, almost knocking him off the bed.

After a few minutes of whimpering, she opened her eyes, her arms wrapped tightly around her body. "I remembered." She took gulps of air. "All of it." Her body shook and sweat covered her face.

He was sure the marriage ceremony, sharing a bed, and the little bit of cuddling they'd done had provoked the dream.

"Do ye wish to talk about it?"

"'Tis what they all thought," she wailed. "I was taken,

abused and I finally escaped. 'Twas horrible." She wiped the sweat from her face with a shaky hand.

"I had been walking in the woods, something I did all the time. He grabbed me from behind and covered my mouth with his hand. He brought me to this small cottage and tied me up." Her hand continued to shake as she pushed her hair from her face. "He left me there and returned several times bringing me food and then he would…"

Callum pulled her into his arms, happy that she allowed it. He would find the mon if it took the rest of his life and make sure he died a painful death. "Do ye think ye remember him enough so that yer brothers and I could find the mon?"

She shook her head. "Nay. That would be impossible."

"'Tis a long time, to be sure, but that doona mean he isna still around here."

She brought her knees to her chin and hugged them to her. "The mon will ne'er be found." She looked up at him with tear-filled eyes, her face as pale as new milk. "I killed him," she whispered. "And I'm going to hell."

12

Callum rubbed her back as she cried in his arms. The darkness in the room was overwhelming, but he dinna want to leave her to light a few candles.

She pushed away from him and rubbed her eyes with the heel of her hands. "Do ye understand? I'm a killer. If anyone finds out I will be hanged."

"Nay, love. 'Tis not true. The only person who can order ye hanged is yer laird and I ken for a fact Haydon would no' do that. Also, if ye were held against yer will and being harmed, any killing was self defense."

So this was what the lass had been suffering with for years. Not only the abuse she endured, but that she killed her tormentor.

Donella began to rock back and forth. "I once asked Father McNeil about killing a mon."

"And what did he say?"

"It was a mortal sin and I would go to hell."

Callum's brows rose. "He told ye that after he kenned

ye had been missing for four days and showed up battered and bruised?"

She shook her head. "Nay. I dinna tell him it was me, I just asked what the punishment would be for killing a mon."

"That doona make sense, lass. Men kill each other in battles all the time."

"I mentioned that, but he said war dinna count because the men were defending their families and homes."

Callum ran his fingers through his hair. Instead of trying to coax Donella closer to him, he began to edge a little bit at a time toward her.

Could it have been the guilt at having a killed a mon that had caused her years of hiding from herself, and everyone else? Definitely no', he was certe. 'Twas most likely both the abuse and killing that caused her to withdraw from everyone.

Donella looked off into the distance. "He came to the cottage one night and once again," she gulped and took a deep breath "he abused me. Then instead of leaving me tied up and the door locked as he did before, he passed out. I believe he was drunk." She hesitated for a moment. "I took the knife at his side and plunged it into his chest. Blood was everywhere. I dinna wait but left the cottage and ran. I had no idea where I was, and my brother found me wandering in the woods." She looked at him, her beautiful blue eyes filled with tears. "I had no idea how long I was gone until they told me." She paused. "Can ye help me, Callum? I doona want to return to what I was before the fall knocked me out."

"Do ye remember now how ye were during that time?"

She nodded. "Ach, yes. During that time, whene'er the picture of me plunging a dagger into the mon flashed in front of my eyes, I moved myself to my safe place. A place where no one kenned I was a murderer. 'Twas much easier to avoid everyone to keep me from yelling out what I had done."

He thought of so many ways to help her, and so many things he could do. Again he moved closer. "Do ye feel settled enough for me to hold ye? Gently."

'Twas easy to see the lass was fighting within herself. He firmly believed she dinna want to return to the way she was before, but still raw from the recent return of her memory, he had to go slowly. But he kenned in his heart if they dinna make a connection now, after her memory had returned, they might ne'er do it.

To his relief, she scooted over until she placed her hand on his chest. She actually smiled. "Do ye ken when we were treating ye for the injury to yer leg, and ye were so burned up with fire, I had to cool ye off by wiping ye down with wet cloths?"

"Aye, I remember yer light, soothing touch."

"What ye dinna ken was that the sight of yer chest and then the rest of ye when we turned ye over brought back some memories."

He reached out and smoothed his palm down her hair. "Bad memories I assume?"

"Aye. Dorathia noticed how my hand shook and tried to get me to leave, but I was determined to help ye and no' go back to the way I was."

"'Twas why ye covered me last night before we fell asleep?"

She smiled. "Aye." Glancing down from his face to his

exposed chest, she said, "With all the other memories racing around my head just now, that doona seem to bother me."

He'd been afraid since she'd awoken that her dream, bringing back her memories, might push her all the way back.

"If yer thinking what I believe ye are, husband, I've had enough good memories since waking up from my fall to ken that I ne'er want to go back to the way I was. The person ye see before ye is the one I was always meant to be. The one I would have turned into naturally had those things no' happened to me."

He opened his mouth to speak, and she held up her hand. "However, I still need yer help. Since I remember everything, I am no' comfortable with what new husbands want."

Whatever disappointment he felt soon turned to the love he had for this woman. With her natural strength, and her desire to have what her brothers have—a normal life—it would only be a matter of time before she became his lover as well as his wife.

"One thing I ask of ye, *mo chridhe*, even though it might no' be easy for ye." He paused for a moment. "Whoever ye are comfortable with in sharing yer memories is up to ye, but I do ask that ye speak again with Father McNeil. From what I understand he will be here for a bit of time."

She took a deep breath. "That would be a hard one."

"Mayhap, but he needs to ken that ye held this in yer heart for years. I am just as sure he will forgive ye as I am that Haydon would no' consider what ye did a hanging offense."

She looked into his eyes and held out her hand. "Hold me, Callum."

* * *

BRIGHT AND EARLY THE next morning, Donella hurriedly dressed and made her way to the chapel to see Father McNeil. 'Twas earlier than most folk were up, but she kenned the priest was always up before dawn to say Mass.

She entered the small building, loving the familiar scent of candles that brought back so many memories from her childhood. Once she'd been found in the woods, she'd avoided church, feeling as though sinners dinna belong there. Her wedding yesterday was the first time she'd been in church in years.

"Good morning, Lady Donella. Or should I be calling ye Lady Donella Gunn?"

She laughed at the mon's cheerful attitude. "Just Donella would be fine, Father."

He waved to a bench along the wall inside the kirk and they both settled there. "What brings the new bride here so early? Surely yer no' wishing to undo yesterday?" He smiled despite his words.

"Nay, Father. I am most pleased with my husband." She hesitated for a moment, not quite sure how to deal with her question. Always starting at the beginning was best.

"Years ago, when I was about fourteen summers, I was kidnapped and held for three days before I escaped, and a day later Haydon found me."

The priest patted her hand. "Aye, I remember, lass. 'Twas a terrible time for yer whole family, especially the laird since he took a great deal of responsibility onto his shoulders for what happened to ye."

"Yet he was so young and newly acting as laird."

"'Tis the way of Laird Haydon, lass. He has always been verra protective of his women, his family and the clan. It took some talking to me about it to get him straightened out."

This was something she dinna ken, but she had been so involved in her own pain and guilt, she hadn't noticed anyone around her. For years.

The time had come to handle something that had tortured her for years. "Father, I was able to escape the mon who held me because—" She stopped and took a deep breath.

"Yes, lass, what is it?"

"I...I killed him."

The priest sat back and closed his eyes. "And ye have carried this burden all these years?"

"Aye. One time shortly after I returned home, I asked ye if killing someone would send ye to hell. And ye said yes."

"Ach, Donella lass, ye ne'er told me why ye were asking that question. If yer looking for forgiveness, ye have it. The good lord donna expect us to not defend ourselves."

"But Jesus dinna defend himself with his captors. As the son of god he could have called the angels to his defense."

Father McNeil shook his head. "Nay. That is no' the same as what yer telling me. God had a plan for his Son and it dinna involve him taking a sword to his enemies." He wagged his finger at her. "Ye need to spend more time with yer Bible, lass."

She truly felt as though a large stone in her heart had melted. She had the forgiveness of Father McNeil and through him the good lord. "So I willna be going to hell?"

He actually laughed. "Well, I canna say that for sure, depending on the rest of yer life. But kenning ye as I do and with the life ye now have planned for yerself with bairns to one day take care of, I doona think ye will be roaming the countryside looking for people to kill."

She let out a big sigh. "Thank ye so much, Father."

"Now, lass, I want ye to return to yer husband, who loves ye verra much." He stopped and grinned. "Aye I could see it in his eyes yesterday. And I could see yer love as well. Take care of each other and put all the bad memories behind ye."

He raised his hand and blessed her.

Donella walked slowly back to the keep deep in thought. Aye, she loved Callum and she kenned he loved her, but she still had to overcome other problems before they could have a normal life together.

He greeted her at the door to the keep when she reached the bottom of the stone steps. "Where were ye, lass? I was afraid ye left me."

She joined her arm in his. "Nay, my love. I willna leave ye. I need ye to help me overcome the remaining problems I have."

They walked into the great hall where clan members and warriors had begun breaking their fast. She noticed the only family member at her table was Ainslee, holding giggling Alasdair on her lap, while trying to keep Susana from dripping her porridge all over her dress.

"Can I help ye, Ainslee?" Donella asked as she walked up to the table.

"Aye, please. Jenny is still not feeling well and the young lass who helped me yesterday is busy serving breakfast."

Donella and Callum took seats. Donella right next to Susana and Callum next to her.

"The new bride and groom are certainly up early," Ainslee said with a grin. She leaned in close to Donella, her eyes on Callum to make sure he was busy with Susana. "Is all well, lass? Last night we heard a disturbance coming from yer bedchamber. Yer brother wanted to investigate, but I told him to leave ye alone."

She smiled. "Do no' fash yerself, e'erything is just fine."

Her sister-by-marriage appeared to want to ask another question, but apparently deciding not to, turned her attention again to Alasdair. "Nay, lad, ye canno' throw porridge at yer sister."

Soon more warriors arrived, some of them looking as though they were feeling the results of the wedding celebration the night before.

Haydon, Conall, and Maura also arrived. By the looks of them, they dinna spend as much drinking and dancing as the rest of them did. But then—she shivered—they had things to keep them busy in their bedchambers.

As she stirred her porridge, playing with it more than eating, Donella thought perhaps now Ainslee would be willing to speak with her about bed activities. She certainly kenned how Callum made her feel when he kissed her and ran his hand up and down her body. 'Twas time to find out what came next so she wasna surprised when they retired tonight.

Aye, she had decided tonight she would try to allow Callum to do more than he'd done the night before. With

Father McNeil's blessing, and her love for her husband, she would do her verra best to let her memories go. 'Twas a long time ago. Then she was no' much more than a child, now she was a married woman with a husband who loved her and would no' force her to do anything she dinna want to do.

* * *

CALLUM COULD FEEL the difference in the air as he and Donella entered their bedchamber. It had been decided they would continue to use her room until the house Callum planned to build was finished. Now that he had Donella's dowry, he could buy what he needed from the villagers to start the house. It would take some time, but at least until then he and his wife had a solid roof over their heads and plenty of food.

Donella had been strangely quiet at the supper they had just shared with her family, the rest of the clan members and warriors. He hadna seen her all day because he'd been on the lists, still in charge of training the new warriors. Conall had said he seemed to have a knack for dealing with the younger lads, giving them confidence without letting them kill each other, or themselves.

She had told him while they were breaking their fast that she'd seen Father McNeil already that morning, but dinna say what they spoke of, although he was most certain it had to be about the guilt she'd carried for years for killing her captor. He only wished the mon wasna dead so he could kill him. Slowly. Painfully.

Donella wandered her bedchamber, looking around as if she hadn't seen it before.

He walked up behind her and placed his hands on her shoulders. When she didn't move or stiffen, he spread her silky hair over her shoulder and kissed the soft pale skin on her neck.

She leaned back against his chest, so he continued across her neck, nibbling on her ear lobe. "Ye are so soft and warm, my love."

"Hmm." She tilted her head so he had more access to her neck. Slowly, he unfastened the back of her gown and slid it off her shoulders. Her bent elbows kept it from dropping to the floor, so he pulled both of her hands down, the garment pooling at her feet.

"*Mo Chridhe*" he whispered. "Ye are so beautiful—and donna argue with me."

She turned in his arms and smiled as she wrapped her arms around his body. "Nay, I'll not argue with ye e'en though I doona believe it."

He pushed her hair back and cupped her cheeks in his large hands. He kissed her gently, then trying his best to keep control, tried once again to enter her mouth. She allowed it, but still after less than a minute, she pulled back.

"Would ye care to move o'er to the bed? I ken we will be much more comfortable there."

Donella hesitated for a moment, and then nodded.

He took her hand, and she stepped over the dress lying on the ground and walked with him to the bed. Thinking 'twas best to remain clothed for a bit, he toed off his boots, removed his stockings and then joined her, his kilt and leine still in place.

"Once again, lass, I want ye to stop me anytime ye feel

uncomfortable or nervous. We have the rest of our lives together so there is no need to rush."

No rush even though he'd been walking around with a stiffened cock for days. But this was his wife, not some leman.

Donella smiled. "I spoke with Ainslee today."

Not sure what that meant, but despite how anxious he was to continue what they'd started, he pulled his lust back in and smiled. "Aye?"

She rested her head on her propped up hand. "Before we married I asked her for advice that most lasses get from their mams before marriage."

'Twas not funny for Donella, so he kept his smile to himself, but could imagine how Ainslee felt about dealing with that question when her own lass was a mere five summers, and many years away from needing that information.

"Did she give ye good advice?"

She shook her head. "Nay. She said in my case I should just let ye lead me."

He pulled her closer and right before he covered her lips with his he said, "'Twas good advice. I can give ye all the instruction ye need."

Still restricted by clothing, Callum was still able to feel Donella's soft curves and plump breasts pressing against him. Using his experience over the years, he kept Donella busy with kisses as he drew her chemise down to reveal her perfect breasts.

"Ach, sweetheart, ye are perfect. He lowered his head and licked one nipple. She stiffened again. "Relax, *mo chridhe*. I willna hurt yet in any way. I will stop anytime ye say."

Dear Lord please doona have her ask me to stop.

"I'm not exactly uncomfortable, Callum, but the feelings in my body are strange. Things I've never felt before."

"Good things, my love?"

"I think so."

He took her breast into his mouth and suckled like a babe.

"Ach, that feels good, husband." Her whispered words slid over him like soft air before a storm.

"It only gets better from here. I promise."

It took some maneuvering, but he managed to get all their clothes off while he distracted her with touches, kisses, and soft words in her ear.

His hand wandered down her body, feeling the woman curves, the softness of her skin, the silkiness of the hair between her legs. When he slid a finger into her wetness, she broke off and moved away.

She covered her breasts with her hands, then drew her legs up in an attempt to protect herself from what she'd experienced before.

"Are ye well, lass?"

She took a deep breath and he never in his life had more respect for someone facing horrors than he did then, watching his wife fighting her fears, trying to have a normal life.

He held his hand out. "Come here, Donella. Let me hold ye. I promise that is all I will do."

Tears leaked from her eyes. "I donna want to stop, Callum. I want to be normal. To give my husband what he wants and desires."

"Ach, wife. What I want more than anything is to have a happy wife. One who is no' afraid of her husband, or his attentions."

She swiped at her cheeks. "Do ye think that will ever happen?"

He kenned nothing more would happen this night and as much as he wished things to be different, he kenned he had to earn her trust in this, so 'twas time to stop. Mayhap once she was asleep, he would take a dive in the cold loch behind the castle.

"Do ye wish to stop?"

She waited for a long moment, then said, "Aye. If ye doona mind."

Mind? His body was about to explode. But some things were more important. 'Twas important for him to make a list of those things while he smiled at his frightened wife.

"Nay. I suggest we just lay together for a while, talk a little bit, and then go to sleep."

The fierce nodding of her head convinced him nothing further would happen that night. He stood, extinguished the candles around the room, then joined her in bed.

By that time Donella had noticeably relaxed and had slid down in the bed, the bedcovers up to her neck.

He had to remind himself that grown men, warriors especially, did not cry.

Laying down, he reached for Donella and she moved over to him. He pulled her close and they snuggled. Holding her naked body next to his was one of the worst things he'd ever had to deal with.

But deal with it he would. The stakes were too high.

13

They'd been married more than three weeks and Callum was growing frustrated. He'd gotten further with his wife, but not far enough. He would never force her, but he would have to push her a bit more. It seemed like she was settling into married life quite nicely but was happy with just their cuddling and slight touches at night.

He was not.

He received sympathetic looks from Conall and Haydon who apparently kenned his dilemma. Most likely Ainslee and Maura kept them up to date on what Donella told them each day as they did their chores around the keep, and she worked with Dorathia.

The poor lads he was training were worn to the bone at the end of the day on the lists. But no matter how hard he pushed himself, he still needed a dunk in the loch's cold water each night after Donella fell asleep.

He dragged himself back to the keep as he was considering taking a dunk before the evening meal and then again later. He would be the cleanest warrior in the Highlands. Probably all of Scotland.

"Callum." Malcolm headed toward him with a missive in his hand. "A rider just brought this for ye. Are ye able to read it?"

Callum took it from his hand. "Aye. My da made sure me and my brother could both read, write, and do our sums. 'Tis been verra helpful."

Malcolm continued past him, most likely headed to his own house where his wife Christine would be preparing the evening meal for them and their bairn. As cousin to Haydon, Malcolm had been given a piece of land from the laird when he'd married Christine, which Malcolm used to build a small, comfortable house for them.

It had also come with tenant farmers who supplied Christine with her eggs, milk, and meat, which left Malcolm free to continue to work on the lists every day.

Haydon had told Callum that soon he would gather a group of warriors to help him build a house for himself and Donella on the land that had come with Donella's dowry. He would earn his living working on the lists, and they would take their meals at the castle where Donella would continue to work with Dorathia to learn healing.

The thought in the back of his mind nudged him again about speaking with Dorathia. He hoped mayhap she could give him some advice, or even speak with Donella to ease some of her fears. But that he would leave until the time came—which he hoped would not—when he could think of nothing else to do to consummate his marriage.

He walked to the edge of the loch and dropped his clothes alongside his sword and dove into the water. 'Twas not as cold as the nighttime when he generally took his swim. It felt good and mayhap a swim before he took Donella to bed each night might work better than just cleaning himself up with soap and water. Hell, he would swim *and* wash with soap and water if it would please his wife.

"Husband, you're going to miss supper if ye doona drag yerself out of that water." Donella stood alongside his clothes, her hands on her hips, a smile on her beautiful face.

Ach, he loved the lass. He would work harder to make her comfortable and at ease with him. He strolled out of the water and instead of turning her head, she continued to stare at him. Actually, one part of him had seemed to garner her attention, which he found quite odd given her fears.

"Why is yer," she waved her hand at his middle, "so small?"

He shook as much water off himself as he could and took his plaid from her hands. "I assume ye mean my man parts?"

She nodded and watched him fold his kilt and wrap it around his waist, fastening it with his belt. After gathering his sword and other weapons he carried on him, he threw his arm over her shoulders and tugged her to him. "Well, ye see, lass, the cold water does that."

"How verra interesting." They started to walk toward the castle when Donella stopped. "What is that on the ground?" She pointed to the missive he'd forgotten about.

He bent and picked it up. "'Tis a missive a rider brought for me today. I forgot about it."

"Ye receive so many, then that 'tis hard to keep them all straight?" she said with a smirk.

"Aye, 'tis quite popular I am." He opened it and stopped as he read the words. He looked up at her with a frown.

* * *

"What is it?" Donella asked. The strangest look had come over Callum's face.

"I'm not sure. All it says is there is an old midwife who lives on the edge of Gunn land—apparently not too far from here—who I should speak with."

Donella looked at the parchment in his hand. "Who sent the note?"

"It doesna say." He took her by the hand, linking their fingers together as they walked to the castle.

"How verra odd."

He frowned at her. "What is odd, lass, is why ye think ye have my permission to leave the castle to come fetch me."

"'Tis a short walk," she said.

"I doesna matter. I doona want ye outside the castle walls. 'Tis dangerous times, and I doona want anything to happen to ye."

She shrugged. He was probably right and after what had happened to her, she should ken better. But she'd been so anxious to see him, learn about his day, tell him about hers, that she dinna think about it.

'Twas her favorite part of marriage. Kenning someone cared to hear about what she did all day and then share his time apart with her.

When she shared that with Ainslee, she told her while that made her happy to hear, she would one day find another thing about marriage that was her favorite time.

She blushed, kenning exactly what her sister-by-marriage meant.

She was trying truly she was, and Callum was being verra patient with her. However, seeing him come out of the loch without any clothes dinna frighten her as it generally did, but brought a strange tingling feeling to her woman parts.

Tonight, she promised herself, she would try harder to let Callum do things to her she hadn't been comfortable with before. If she wanted to have a bairn or two—which she did—she would have to move beyond her fears.

The great hall was as noisy as ever as the warriors poured into the space and took their seats as the serving lasses carried out trays of food and placed them on the tables, bantering back and forth with the men.

Callum and Donella joined the family on the dais. Holding Finlay in her lap, Ainslee filled a trencher for Susana and Alasdair as Haydon wrestled with Grace who sat on is lap and was trying to grab everything within her reach.

"Can I help ye, Ainslee?" Donella asked.

"Aye, if ye can take Grace from Haydon, that would help. He's no' paying enough attention to her and look at the mess she's making."

"I take it Nancy is still ill?"

"Aye. But Dorathia visited with her this afternoon and said the lass will be back on her feet tomorrow. Canna be too soon for me," she said. "I love my bairns, but four of them at the same time, trying to feed them here instead of the nursery is a challenge."

"My lady, as soon as I am finished serving, I can take

them upstairs to the nursery for the rest of the evening and get them ready for bed."

With a bright smile and a deep sigh as she grabbed Grace's hand, Ainslee said to Dana, one of the young servers, "Thank ye. I would appreciate that verra much."

Callum began to fill their trencher with the roasted venison and stewed vegetables. Loaves of warm bread, hard cheese, and boiled eggs were also laid out on dishes the lasses placed before them.

"Ye seem distracted tonight," Donella said.

"Aye. I'm still confused by the missive I received."

"Do ye ken this midwife? What did the missive say her name was?"

"Old Marta, the note said. Nay, I dinna ken her. When I lived at the Gunn Castle we had a healer by the name of Ceit and she did the midwifing. I doona ever remember anyone by the name of Marta."

"Will ye go to her, then?"

He shrugged. "Since she's on Gunn land, I'm a tad leery about going there. Remember, I was banned, which means if I am caught, Fraser has the right to have me executed."

Donella sucked in a deep breath. "Nay! He wouldna do that!"

Apparently overhearing their conversation, Conall turned to Donella. "The mon set yer husband up as a fumbling warrior, which I ken no' to be true, and then banned him from the clan. I would say, aye, he would have him executed."

She shivered, thinking about Fraser Gunn. What a terrible mon he must be. Callum and Conall had begun to discuss the note Callum had received and Donella turned her thoughts inward. With the love and support she'd always had from her brothers and her sisters-by-marriage, she couldna imagine a sibling doing to Callum what Fraser had done.

She liked the fact that both Haydon and Conall trusted Callum and admired his skill with a sword. The fact that Conall said he kenned that Callum had been set up meant a lot to her.

"I think tomorrow after I leave the lists, I will go to see this midwife."

Donella shook her head. "Nay."

"Why no'? I'm curious to see someone I donna ken. A midwife."

"I'm no' saying ye shouldn't go, I'm saying *we* will go see this woman. Both of us. Together."

"Nay. 'Tis too dangerous. This could be some sort of a trap."

Conall leaned forward. "Yer husband is right, Donella, Ye canno' go traipsing to Gunn land. First of all, as yer husband said, it could be a trap. I doona trust his brother." He looked at Callum. "I will go with ye."

"As will I," Haydon, who Donella hadna even realized was listening to them, said.

Ainslee placed her hand on Donella's arm. "'Tis best to leave these things to the men."

Haydon reached out his hand to Callum. "I only heard part of yer conversation. I'd like to see this note."

Callum handed it over and leaned back, his arms crossed over his chest as he watched the laird read it. "Do ye ken who this woman is?" Haydon asked.

"Nay," Callum said. "As I told Donella, the only healer,

who also worked as midwife at Gunn Castle, was Ceit Gunn."

Haydon handed the note back to Callum and nodded. "We ride at first light. We will take six more warriors with us."

* * *

CALLUM SMOOTHED Donella's hair back from her forehead as she laid in his arms. They were both unclothed and had done some verra serious kissing and touching. Although he would have liked it to go a bit further, he was distracted by tomorrow's trip to the midwife he was asked to visit.

At first he'd dismissed it as trivial, almost a prank by one of the other warriors, but then when they'd begun to discuss it at the table and Conall and then Haydon had joined in, he'd realized this could indeed be a trap by his brother.

Since Fraser had sent a request to negotiate a marriage contract with Donella and was turned down, he could hold resentment not only toward him, but Sutherlands, as well.

Certainly word of their marriage had reached his brother by now.

The clans were joined at one part of Sutherland land. Since they were no' at war, even though there was no friendliness between them, the two clans had no' stopped clansmen from crossing the border from one side to the other.

Fraser could verra well have sent the note to take his revenge on him, leaving Donella free to marry him.

He looked down at Donella who had fallen asleep, her small hand resting on his chest. 'Twas time to leave for his dip in the loch.

THE SUN HAD BARELY BROKEN over the horizon when Callum, Conall, and Haydon strode to the stable to fetch their horses. Haydon had requested Malcolm to remain behind since they weren't verra sure what they were riding into and what might have been planned for the castle while they were gone.

The six warriors Haydon had selected to ride with them were already there, tacking their mounts.

Callum looked down again at the note in his hand. Besides the name of the midwife, it had vague directions on how to find the woman.

Haydon raised his arm, and the men rode out of the castle, the thundering of the horses across the wooden drawbridge echoing around them.

'Twas a cool morning, but with the summer coming to an end, expected.

Callum was curious about this midwife someone thought he should speak with, and honored that the laird thought it important enough to travel with him and bring warriors as well.

They rode freely, enjoying the morning air while on Sutherland land. When they crossed over the border to Gunn territory, they were more cautious, watching their surroundings more carefully.

Haydon rode up next to Callum. "I doona think 'tis a good idea for us all to ride up to this woman's cottage.

Just in case 'tis no' a trap we doona want to scare the midwife to death before she has said anything."

"I prefer to go alone to the cottage, but I also doona want to walk into my death, either." Callum grinned at Haydon. "I promised yer sister I would return to her."

"I will go with ye to the cottage. The other men will surround the place but hidden so as not to cause the old woman stress."

Conall rode up to Callum's other side. "Did the directions in the note mean anything to ye?"

"Aye. Now that we're here, memories are coming back to me. As lads Fraser and I would play in the woods behind the castle. One day we wandered farther away than we were supposed to. I remember we found this cottage and there was a woman living there. We teased each other that she was a witch and would cast a spell on us.

"She chased us away with her broom, and seemed to ken our names which was odd since we hadn't e'er seen her before."

"Think ye that woman is the same midwife who someone wanted ye to speak with?"

"Aye," Callum said. "I am certes it is her. 'Tis too much of a coincidence. In fact, 'twas after that happened when Fraser began to turn on me. We had been the best of friends, but he went into training a year before me, and from then we ne'er seemed to have the same friendship."

"Since he falsely accused ye of causing yer da's death and then banned ye from yer clan, I would say that friendship had, indeed, ended."

About two hours later, Callum took in his surroundings and came to a halt. "'Tis only about a mile from here."

They rode carefully and quietly until they spotted the cottage. It sat in the midst of a cove of trees. Smoke from a peat fire rose from the chimney. A verra large garden in front of the house held herbs and flowers. Along the side a tidy garden of vegetables grew.

Haydon waved his arms for the men to spread out as he and Callum walked to the front of the cottage, their hands resting on their swords.

Before Callum could knock, the door opened. Many years older, but he still recognized the woman who they had met while playing in the woods that day.

"Ach, Callum Gunn," she said in a soft melodious voice, opening the door wider. "'Ye finally came to hear what I had to say."

They both had to duck their heads to enter the cottage. 'Twas a small space, clean and cozy. A fire burned in the small fireplace, a few chairs, an old, worn table, and a cot in the corner were the only furniture pieces.

"And ye, of course, are Laird Haydon Sutherland," she said as she waved them to the two chairs. "Have a seat, and I will pour us some ale." She stopped and turned, a sly smile on her face. "Unless ye prefer a bit of whisky. The castle sends me some once in a while."

"Nay, no ale or whisky," Haydon said. "Are ye the one who sent the note to Callum?"

She looked at Callum with a warm smile. "Ye turned into a fine mon. I kenned it when I saw ye and Fraser all those years ago. I dinna send the note, but asked the lad who brings me things from the castle to write it and bring it to ye. 'Tis getting close to the end of my time here and I wanted to make sure ye kenned what ye needed before I die."

"Are ye ill, then?" Callum asked.

"Nay. But at my age ye ne'er ken for sure if ye will wake up once ye close yer eyes." She cackled like Callum remembered when he was a boy. 'Twas why he and Fraser teased each other about her being a witch.

Callum leaned forward in the chair, his fingers linked between his knees. "What did ye want to see me about, Marta?"

"'Tis a secret I've held for years, but as I said, with the years passing, I had to let ye ken. Then when I heard what yer brother did by banning ye from the clan, I had to find a way to ease my soul before I took my final journey."

Callum walked over to the woman where she sat on the cot. He knelt before her and took her hands in his. "What is the secret, Marta Gunn?"

She stared at him for a full minute. "The wrong mon sits in the laird's chair at Gunn Castle."

14

Donella tapped on Dorathia's door and peeked in. "Are ye free for a few minutes, Dorathia?"

"Aye, lass, come in." She was just finishing up her breakfast of oatcakes and apples. "I have a few more oatcakes if ye are wanting one."

"Nay, thank ye, but I just finished breaking my fast." She pulled up a stool and settled next to the healer who was already sorting herbs to be made into potions. "Can I ask ye something?"

Dorathia put the leaves into the bowl and began crushing them. "Of course." She looked at her, stopping her work for a second. "If I am able."

Donella picked up a pile of herbs and began to separate them into piles. "I love Callum verra much."

Dorathia smiled as she worked her pestle. "Aye."

"And he loves me, too."

She nodded. "There is no one in the keep who doona ken it with the way ye look at each other." She grinned as she continued to pound the leaves into powder. "If ye came here to tell me what I already ken—what everyone already kens—then I could use yer help and we can chat."

Donella took a deep breath. "Can ye explain to me how the marriage act works if yer not being forced?"

Dorathia stopped her pounding and looked at her with a curious, but sad look. "Ach, it sounds like the bride is still having problems."

"Aye." Donella sighed and placed her hands in her lap. "I want verra much to let Callum make love to me, but I remember my time with the hated mon as bloody and painful. I ken Callum would ne'er hurt me, but if I kenned exactly how it would go when yer with someone ye love, it might help me."

The healer picked up her mug of ale and finished it off. "I will be happy to help ye, lass, but have ye talked to Lady Sutherland, or Maura?"

She shook her head. "Before I married, Ainslee told me 'twas better if my husband just led me. As much as I would love to try to talk to one of them now that I've been married for a while, they are always distracted with their bairns and jobs around the castle. Also, I donna want to take a chance of anyone overhearing me. 'Twould not be good for word to leak out that such a braw handsome warrior as Callum hasn't bedded his wife yet."

"Verra true."

Feeling more comfortable speaking of the matter without having to look Dorathia right in the eye, Donella picked up more herbs and began to slide her fingers over them to release the small leaves. "Callum and I lie together each night unclothed. He had insisted on that almost from the start."

Dorathia merely nodded.

"We do some touching and kissing and it feels so good that I ken there is more that will also feel good, but then the memory comes back of the pain the horrid mon caused."

Dorathia laid her pestle down and took both of Donella's hands in hers. "When Callum kisses ye and touches ye in certain spots, do ye feel yerself grow wet in yer woman's parts?"

Donella blushed so hard she was sure her head would explode. "Aye."

"That is yer body preparing itself for Callum. Believe me, lass, the mon kens what he is doing. Also, with as much as he loves ye, he would certainly make verra sure ye were ready before he tried to complete the act."

Donella slumped on the stool. "Ye make it sound easy," she whispered with a shaking voice.

Dorathia patted her hand. "With the mon ye love 'tis not just easy, but wonderful."

They continued to work at the table while Donella thought about what Dorathia had said. Both Ainslee and Maura have told her the marriage bed was a wonderful place and with Ainslee popping out four bairns in six years, she must be right.

She pounded the herbs in her mortar and decided this would be the night she would allow her husband to show her how wonderful it could be.

'Twas close to the nooning when the sound of horses riding over the drawbridge drew Donella's attention. "It sounds like the men have returned."

She had told Dorathia that Callum had received a vague note and he, Haydon, Conall and six warriors had ridden out at dawn to learn what it was all about.

"I will return, Dorathia. I must see what Callum has discovered."

"Go, lass. 'Tis time for the nooning anyway."

Donella brushed her hands on her skirts and left the small cottage. The men were dismounting, and the grooms were taking their horses away.

She walked up to Callum. "Did ye learn anything?"

He reached out and placed his hand on her head and smoothed her hair. "Aye. Haydon wants to call a meeting after the nooning and we will speak of it then."

"A meeting?"

"Aye." He wrapped his arm around her shoulders and moved her toward the dais where the other family members had gathered.

The room soon filled with warriors and other clan members who ate at the castle.

Large bowls of vegetable stew, warm loaves of bread and sweet butter had Donella's stomach growling. Callum filled their trencher, and she tore off pieces of bread for each of them.

"Ye are no' going to tell me anything?" She dipped her bread into her stew.

"Nay. The laird wants to handle it his way."

The laird? That confused her. Why would Haydon be involved in something that apparently concerned Callum? Her husband hadn't arrived back with a sword to his back, so whatever it was, 'twas most likely not bad news.

The warriors were noisy, but the family members on the dais ate quietly. Jenny had risen from her sick bed, so the bairns were now taking their meals again in the nursery.

Maura and Ainslee kept glancing sideways at their

husbands, most likely just as curious as she was to find out what had happened. It dinna appear as if there had been a battle.

Patience. That was what she needed, which she would have if they would all just hurry up.

* * *

THEY ASSEMBLED in Haydon's solar. All family members were present. Haydon, Ainslee, Callum, Donella, Conall, Maura, Malcolm, and Christine.

Callum reached over and took Donella's hand in his, giving it a squeeze. He had no idea what would come of this meeting or what the laird had planned, since Haydon hadn't spoken about it since they'd left Old Marta's cottage. All he said was "we will meet with the family and discuss this."

Once everyone was settled, all attention was focused on Haydon.

"Although this matter involves Callum, as a member of Clan Sutherland, through his pledge to me when he joined us, and now husband to my sister, this complicated matter needs to be presented to us all.

"I ken that most times these kinds of situations are generally handled solely by the men, leaving the women out, but I believe 'tis in everyone's best interest to hear what Callum has to say and what we will do about it." He turned to Ainslee. "Plus my lovely wife taught me years ago that women have a lot to contribute."

The silence was deafening, the only sounds in the room was everyone breathing. Haydon nodded to Callum. "'Tis yer story to tell, brother."

He tried his best to repeat what they'd heard. Taking a deep breath, he said, "As ye all ken, we visited with a midwife on the Gunn property this morning after receiving a note saying I should see her.

"Old Marta was the midwife who helped bring my brother, Fraser into the world. In the midst of the pain and suffering my mam endured, she admitted to the midwife that my da had not fathered the bairn she was delivering. She told old Marta that she was already carrying Fraser when she married The Gunn."

Donella took in a deep breath as every pair of eyes in the room focused on Callum.

"What does that mean?" Donella asked.

"Let yer husband finish, sister."

Callum ran his fingers through his hair. "Once the bairn was born, my mam made Old Marta swear ne'er to tell anyone. However, not trusting the midwife, she had her sent to the cottage at the edge of the Gunn property. Although she was ne'er allowed to work again as a midwife, my mam made sure she was provided for over the years."

"That means," Ainslee said, looking at her husband.

"Callum is the rightful Laird of Gunn." Haydon answered her unasked question.

"Does Fraser ken this?" Donella asked.

Callum stood and began to pace. "I had time to think on this while we rode back, and I have a feeling he does. When we were lads, we roamed the land and were verra close. One day we stumbled upon the cottage where Old Marta lives. She was much younger then, of course, but she took great notice of the two of us and even called us by name.

"Did she say anything that made ye question what ye discovered today?" Christine asked.

"Nay." Callum continued his pacing. "However, it was right after that when things changed between Fraser and me. We no longer played together, and he was put into sword training. Since I was younger, I was not. Shortly after that, he was sent to Mackay to train under their laird."

Donella turned to Haydon. "Is Callum truly the rightful heir of Clan Gunn?"

"Aye." Haydon was now the one running his fingers through his hair. "It seems he is. The question is, does Fraser ken this?" He nodded at Callum. "In my opinion, I think he does which would explain why he accused ye of causing yer da's death and then banning ye."

"I always wondered what the reason was for doing such a thing," Malcolm said.

Callum leaned against the wall and crossed his arms over his chest. With all he'd heard that morning, and then remembering things from his childhood, he'd spent the ride back to the castle going back and forth between anger and an odd sort of pity for his brother.

"Since 'tis almost certes that yer brother kens, how did he find out?" Malcolm asked.

Callum shook his head. "I'm no' sure. When we returned home, I remembered us going to Mam and telling her about our adventure. Since it meant nothing then, I now realize she seemed quite nervous, and spent a great deal of time asking us questions about our visit. Then she forbade us from e'er going to see the woman again."

The room grew quiet, until finally Haydon said, "'Tis

yer right to hold the title Laird of Gunn. 'Tis also yer right to take over the castle and rule the clan by whatever means."

Callum puffed out a breath and looked at the ceiling. "However, one little thing we are missing. I pledged my loyalty to ye, Haydon, and married my wife in Sutherland plaid."

"Aye, ye did, but ye dinna ken what ye ken now."

He was so mixed up he felt as if his insides were twisted in knots. He now kenned why his brother did what he did by accusing him and then using that as an excuse to ban him. He must have feared he would somehow discover their mam's secret.

"You mentioned that yer relationship with yer brother turned when ye told yer mam the story about your visit with Old Marta. That makes me think that afterward yer mam told Fraser the truth and encouraged him to continue to think of himself as the future laird and suggested he break from ye in case he slipped and told ye the truth."

"How long since yer mam passed?" Maura asked.

"Ten years or so."

The room grew silent once again. Then Conall looked at Haydon. "What is to be done?"

Haydon looked at Callum. "'Tis yer decision. Ye are the rightful Laird of Gunn. We support whatever decision ye make. However, I suggest we confront The Gunn with this information and hear what he has to say about it."

Callum thought about the problem. He was happy here, as was his wife. He was ne'er one to crave leadership. That, mayhap had to do with the fact that he'd always kenned he would be his brother's second-in-command and would only become laird if his brother passed before he did.

No' only had his mam cheated him out of his rightful position, Fraser had set him up, and then banned from the clan to assure his position.

He looked over at Donella, his beautiful and loving wife. Anger built when he thought about how the mon had tried to snatch Donella away from him by asking Haydon to consider marriage arrangements between him and his wife. After the scuffle in the alehouse, Fraser had to ken that Callum was living here and courting Donella.

'Twas quite sad to realize how verra much his brother hated him.

"There is no way I can live peacefully with myself if I let Fraser get away with this. I am the rightful Laird of Gunn and 'tis time I stepped up and took my proper place."

Haydon nodded at him. "I agree. Now we must decide how to handle it. I prefer no' to wage war on the Gunn, but if it comes to that, we stand behind ye."

Callum returned to his seat and wrapped his arm around Donella and pulled her close to him. "What think ye, wife?"

"Whatever ye wish to do. I am with Haydon, that ye should claim yer proper place."

"I believe 'tis best to invite Fraser here for a meeting. Maybe have Old Marta present to repeat her story in front of him. I doona want him to ken what is on my mind until he arrives since I have no idea what he will do if he finds out before he comes."

Haydon nodded. "I will send a missive to the mon

asking him to come for a meeting here. I won't say it, but make it sound like a border issue."

"Aye, 'tis better to have him here at Dornoch before I confront him."

"I shall send a mon out with the message now and suggest a meeting in two days. I doona want to give him too much time to consider why I'm asking, since I turned down his request for a betrothal between him and Donella," Haydon said as he stood, indicating the meeting had come to an end.

Callum, Malcolm and Conall headed to the lists to put in a few hours before they stopped for the day. Right now he needed the exercise to work off his anger and resentment.

* * *

Two days later, Donella reached over in the bed and felt the empty space. 'Twas no longer warm, which meant Callum had arisen a while before.

She thew off the covers and shivered as the cool air hit her skin. The early fall weather was making its presence known.

Quickly dressing, she pulled on warm stockings and leather shoes and left the room. She grabbed her wrap on the way out.

She found Callum pacing at the bottom of the stairs. He looked up and granted her an amazing smile. "Be careful coming down, lass. As much as I enjoy holding ye in my arms, I doona wish to repeat our first meeting."

Donella reached the last step and Callum drew her close to his body. "Good morn, wife."

"Good morn, husband."

They grinned at each other and then he took her mouth in a toe-curling kiss.

"Enough of that, we must get ready for our meeting." Haydon walked past them, nudging Callum in the arm.

"If ye wish to break yer fast before Fraser arrives, I suggest ye do it now," Haydon said as he headed to the great hall.

"Is he close?" Donella asked.

"Aye, our rider returned about a quarter hour ago and said he and his party were about half an hour away."

Donella and Callum took a seat at a table in the kitchen and ate bread and cheese and sipped on warmed ale.

"Riders have arrived." The call echoed around the great hall and reached the kitchen. Callum stood and reached out for Donella's hand.

Fingers linked, they walked to the great hall where Haydon stood, his hands behind his back, with Conall and Malcolm standing next to him, slightly back.

Callum studied her face with concern. "Mayhap ye should go to Ainslee's solar and wait there in case this gets rough."

"Nay. I want to look the mon in the face who tried to cheat my husband out of his due."

With a great deal of flourish, the mon who Donella assumed was Lord Gunn walked into the great hall, three men behind him. He removed his helmet and pushed his hair back from his forehead.

Donella covered her mouth and her scream echoed around the keep.

Haydon, Callum and Conall all stared in her direction.

"What is it, lass?" Callum said, grasping her shoulders.

Without saying a word, Donella pulled herself free of Callum's grip and raced forward, using all her weight to throw herself on the mon, taking him unaware, so they both tumbled to the ground. She began punching and hitting him as the tears ran down her face.

"I killed ye!! How can ye still be alive, ye bastard?"

15

Callum raced to Donella, pulling her up. He wrapped his arm around his squirming, fidgeting wife's waist and held her as she screamed, kicked, and attempted to fling herself from her husband. He could barely speak, his words roughened by the dryness in his throat. "Fraser is the one who kidnapped ye?"

He turned at the sound of Haydon, Conall, and Malcolm drawing their swords. He walked back with a sobbing Donella and pulled her tight against his chest.

His heart thundered and he felt as if he would bring up the small breakfast they'd just eaten. Fraser was the mon who kidnapped Donella, violated her, beat her, and then was supposedly stabbed to death? He shook his head. The things he'd heard in the last few days were enough to bring him to his knees.

Haydon placed his hand in front of Conall as he moved forward, his sword raised. "Halt!" He nodded to two warriors who had been inside the keep. "Get their swords."

Apparently realizing he was definitely outnumbered and in danger, Fraser did nothing as one of the warriors took his sword. The three other men with him lost their swords as well.

Haydon looked as white-faced as Callum felt. Conall dinna appear much better.

"What is this, Sutherland? Who is this lass and why is she screeching like a banshee?" Fraser said, his hands on his hips. "And I doona ken why ye would take our swords. I thought this was to be a meeting, not a capture. Are ye declaring war against the Gunns?" He pointed at Callum. "So this is where ye ended up, traitor."

Callum handed off Donella to Malcolm and stepped forward. "Ye kenned I was here, *brother*, and doona try to deny it."

He tried verra hard not to run his brother through but managed to hold onto his temper. "Years ago, my wife, Lady Donella Sutherland was kidnapped and held for a mon's pleasure for three days before she escaped. The mon was ne'er found and she now says the mon was ye."

Fraser waved his hand. "Do no' be ridiculous. I ne'er saw the lass before in my life. Besides which, she's screaming that she killed whoever that mon was." He straightened his shoulders and held out his hands. "Think ye I look dead?"

Callum ran his hand down his face. He'd promised himself if they ever found the mon who'd done that damage to Donella, he would tear him apart piece by piece. Now he was looking at his own brother who was being accused, and yet Donella still claimed that she had killed her captor.

He'd ne'er been so shaken and twisted into knots in his life.

"Take them to one of the empty bedchambers," Haydon barked at the warriors holding the Gunn men. He nodded at Callum. "Bring yer wife upstairs and have Ainslee calm her. Then meet us at the dais."

Callum left with a shaking Donella on his arm. She kept insisting, "I killed him. I ken I killed him. I stabbed him in the chest with his own knife."

He hated the idea of leaving her with Ainslee, but the entire thing was such a mess he was grateful to follow Haydon's instructions because his brain seemed to have frozen. This was no' like a battlefield. That he could handle with his eyes closed.

This was betrayal, lies, mistrust, abuse... He couldn't get his thoughts together, but now his main concern had to be Donella. They reached Ainslee's solar, and Callum knocked and was bid enter.

"God's toes, what the devil is going on down there?" Ainslee put aside mending she was working on. Maura sat alongside her, mending also crushed in her hands. Both women were white as ghosts.

Callum swiped his hand over his face. "To tell ye the truth, my lady, I'm no' sure. The laird wishes Donella to stay up here with ye right now."

Donella pulled away from him. "I doona understand, Callum. I killed him. I ken I did." Her entire body continued to shake.

He was torn. He really hated leaving her in this state, but he was needed downstairs. If it was his brother who had done that damage to a young Donella, Callum would indeed take him apart piece by piece. If Haydon and Conall hadn't done so before he returned.

He gave her one more hug and looked over her head at Ainslee. "Take care of her. Send for a warm mug of ale, or a glass of whisky. I will be back as soon as I can." With a soft, yet passionate kiss, he strode from the room and returned to the great hall.

Feeling a tad sturdier since he'd had time to digest all that had happened a few minutes ago, he joined his family.

Seated at the dais, Haydon, Conall, and Malcolm huddled together, speaking in soft voices. They looked up as Callum joined them.

"How is Donella?" Haydon asked.

"Upset, shaky, but in good hands with Ainslee and Maura."

He nodded and said, "After we eat, I want to continue this in my solar. Since we are dealing with the Gunn Laird, and so far we have proof of nothing, I willna toss him into the dungeon or otherwise treat him with disrespect."

He held up his hand as Callum started to speak, enraged that Haydon would forget what Donella had accused Fraser.

"I ken what yer thinking, Callum, but Donella insists she killed the mon who took her. With her saying that, we have to go slow with accusing yer brother of that crime."

After giving instructions to one of the serving lasses to bring food and drink to Gunn and his men, the four Sutherlands ate their meal with quiet and solemness.

On the way to Haydon's solar, Callum stopped at

Ainslee's solar to check on Donella. When she saw him, she stood and held out her hands.

He walked to her and wrapped her in his arms. "It will be well. Just hold on for a while until we get this all straightened out."

She looked up at him, her beautiful eyes filled with tears. "I killed him, Callum, I ken I did."

He smoothed her hair back. "Did ye have anything to calm ye? Should I send to Dorathia for a potion?"

"Nay. I had some whisky, and I do feel a tad better."

"Good. I will return as quickly as possible." He kissed her on the head and left the room.

He heard her mumble, "I killed him."

'Twas a strained group of men who had gathered in Haydon's solar. Once Callum joined them, Haydon spoke. "'Tis a verra strange position we are in now. We invited The Gunn here to discuss his theft of the lairdship and then Donella accuses him of being the mon who kidnapped, abused and violated her." He ran his fingers through his hair.

"Did ye ken before today that she claimed to have killed the mon who took her?" Haydon asked Callum.

"Aye. She said so when her memories of the time with the mon returned. Apparently one of the issues that had troubled her during the period when she wasna herself, was she thought she was going to hell because she killed her captor."

"Did she tell ye anything else that might help?"

"Nay. I feel whatever she told me was either all she remembered or only wanted to talk about." He looked around the table at the men seated there. "I doona want to make anything more difficult for her. She is just now starting to come to grips with what happened to her now that she remembered."

"I would have appreciated it if ye had told me her memory of the time had returned," Haydon groused.

No' daunted by his attitude, Callum said, "'Twas my decision to keep it between us because her feelings were still quite raw." He stared at Haydon. "Donella is yer sister, but she is my *wife*."

"And I am her *laird*."

After several seconds of mon cage rattling, Haydon continued, "If Donella is correct, we now have two charges against the mon."

"My suggestion would be to kill him and solve both problems at the same time," Conall said.

Haydon shook his head. "Despite our feelings on the matter, we cannot take out a laird without positive proof of our charges and permission from our king or we could be looking at full out war. The new king, Charles II has made it clear he doesna want fighting among the clans."

After a few minutes of silence, Malcolm said, "Donella says she stabbed him in the chest, isna that so?"

Callum nodded. "Aye."

"Well, all we need do is have the mon remove leine shirt and we can see if there is a stab wound there."

Callum waved his hand. "Nay. My brother is a warrior. He's been in many battles and could easily have a stab wound on his chest. In fact, I'm sure he does. As we all do."

After a few minutes of silence, Haydon said, "I ken yer not going to like this, Callum, but we need to question

Donella. She is making a serious charge, and one that will give any one of us the right to kill the mon, Charles be damned."

Callum started to shake his head when Haydon first began to speak. His wife was in verra bad shape when he last saw her and he was not about to bring it all back again.

Depending on how any questioning went, it could verra well send her back to what she called her "safe place" and she might never recover again.

"I ken ye were emphatic that Donella is your wife," Haydon said, "but as her laird, I insist that she will be questioned." He held his hand up when Callum began to speak. "However, I will question her without everyone else present. If ye wish to stay with her, ye can do that."

Realizing he had no choice, Callum said. "Aye, I understand. And aye, I will stay with her. Also, if things get too out of hand, brother and laird or no, I will take her from this room. With my sword if I must."

His head pounded with all the events of the past couple of days. He dinna care about the Gunn lairdship as much as he cared if his brother had been the one to destroy Donella's life. And then to have the arrogance to request her hand in marriage!

Haydon stood. "Let us get this o'er with." He stretched his muscles and said, "Callum, fetch Donella and bring her here. The rest of ye can return to the lists. The warriors aren't getting any stronger with us all sitting on our arses."

* * *

Donella should not have had as much whisky as she had. The first few sips had settled her, but now halfway through the mug she was only feeling tired and weepy.

And wanting Callum in the worst way. She needed him. To hold her. To tell her everything would be all right.

As if my magic, he appeared at the door, walking directly to her. He got down on his knees and took her hands. "How are ye, sweetheart?"

Her eyes filled with tears and she nodded. "I am well. I am just so glad to see ye."

He stood and pulled her up, holding her to his chest. Why couldn't life be good to her for once? She'd found the most wonderful mon in the world and now her past was coming back to torture her again.

Almost as if he read her mind, he said, "Doona let this trouble ye. I will stand with ye and we will fight this together. Ye are no' alone, Donella. Ye have many people who love ye, but no' like I do."

She nodded, wiping her eyes with her palms. "What happens now?"

Callum took a deep breath, and she kenned the news coming was no' good. "Haydon wants to speak with ye. He is angry that I ne'er told him ye had regained yer memory about what happened to ye."

She wrapped her arms around Callum's waist. "'Tis glad I am that ye ne'er told him." She looked up. "I guess we should go speak with him and get this o'er with."

Haydon was sitting at his desk, his fingers linked and resting on his stomach. He smiled when she entered, but since she kenned what he wanted, she found it difficult to smile back.

"Doona worry, little one. I only want to ask a few questions. Callum can stay here with ye."

She nodded, suddenly feeling like a young lass facing her brother over some miscreant she was guilty of instead of a grown married woman.

"Callum says ye remembered what happened to ye."

She nodded.

"What makes ye for certes that the mon who came today, Laird Gunn was the mon who kidnapped ye and held ye for a few days?"

She leaned forward, anger taking some of her fear away. "Think ye that he would be someone I'd forget?"

Callum took her hand in his.

"Aye, I understand, but ye keep insisting ye killed the mon."

"I did. He'd fallen asleep after too much drink. I stole his knife from him and stabbed him in the chest. There was a great deal of blood."

"Did ye stay long enough to ken if he was still alive?"

"Nay. I ran for my life. Then I got lost and wandered around until ye found me and brought me home."

'Twas obvious Haydon was trying to get as much information out of her without upsetting her too much. She, on the other hand was no' getting upset, but angry. Somewhere deep inside she kenned she was a strong woman. Dead, or no' Laird Gunn was the mon who took her, abused and beat her and she then killed while he slept. She sighed, e'en to herself that sounded wrong.

"Donella, ye will need to face The Gunn and make yer accusations. In the meantime, we need to treat the mon and his men as guests until we have some proof that he was the mon who kidnapped ye. We also have the problem of addressing him about taking the lairdship from his brother. It must be assumed that unless we have proof, he dinna ken his father was not The Gunn who fathered Callum, making yer husband the rightful Laird of Gunn."

She lifted her chin. "I can face him whene'er I need to."

Both Callum and Haydon smiled at her.

"I think she's had enough for today, Laird. I want to bring her upstairs and have her rest for the afternoon."

Donella shook her head, becoming more and more annoyed at how they treated her, like she was a bairn. Aye, she had fallen apart when she'd first seen Laird Gunn, but all those years of hiding and suffering were o'er. She would face the mon and look him in the eye and have him deny what he'd done to her.

"I doona need to rest for the day. However, I would appreciate some food to dry up the whisky Ainslee fed me." She smiled at Callum. "Will ye join me?"

He returned her smile with one that turned her insides to mush. "I would love to, lass, but I have duties this afternoon. I will see ye this evening." He took her hands in his. "Ye are a strong woman, Donella. Ye will be just fine."

"Aye, I ken. I'm no' longer going to hide behind ye, husband, but stand alongside ye."

She noticed Haydon watching the two of them verra closely. But before she could think about that, she said, "Are ye finished, Laird? I'm going to the kitchen and have Jonet give me something to eat. I will then go see Dorathia and help her."

Looking carefully at her, he said, "Aye. Whatever I need we can discuss tomorrow."

Donella nodded and stood, brushing her skirts. Then

she turned and left the room. The days of everyone taking care of her were o'er.

Dorathia was away from her cottage, most likely attending to a patient. With time on her hands, Donella wandered over to the stables. Angus, Jonet's son, had been named stablemaster a few years ago when the old mon who'd been in charge of the stable for years took to his bed and died within days.

"Angus, I saw ye working with one of the lads who isna old enough to start training. Ye were showing him how to throw a knife."

Angus grinned. "Aye. Young Brandon was interested in doing some sort of weaponry while he waited for the laird to accept him into warrior training."

She nodded. "I want ye to train me, too."

Instead of laughing, the mon looked curious as he rubbed his chin with his thumb and index finger. "Is there a reason ye want to learn that lass? It doesna have anything with yer new husband, does it?"

Donella laughed. "Nay. I love Callum." She dinna want to tell the mon that she wanted to learn more about knives in case she had to kill Gunn again.

"I just want to ken something besides mending and other women's chores." If she told Angus she wanted to learn for any other reason than what she just told him, he would most likely go straight to Haydon and tell him.

"Do ye have a knife, lass?"

Her shoulders slumped. "Nay. Only my eating knife."

He thought for a minute then said, "That wouldn't do. I have a few good, sturdy knives needing sharpening back here that ye can use. If yer looking to protect yerself, which is a good idea for all women, I have a few tricks I can teach ye besides throwing a knife at someone."

She grinned. "That's wonderful. Can we start now?"

16

After leaving the Lists and then taking a swim in the loch, Callum stopped in the room where his brother was housed.

The Gunn and his men were still being held in one of the bedchambers since Haydon dinna want to give the mon the chance to leave until they straightened out the charges against him.

Callum had dodged the questions Fraser had and realized after a few minutes that there really wasn't much reason for his visit since there wasn't anything for the brothers to speak about.

If Old Marta was to be believed, Fraser had conspired with their mam and cheated Callum out of his birthright, and if Donella was correct, his brother had wreaked havoc on her life. Add to that setting Callum up and then banning him from the clan. Those subjects dinna make for friendly conversation.

Callum only grew angrier with his brother as he blathered on about being treated disrespectfully, all the time thinking he might be the one who had violated his wife. The only thing keeping him from beating the life out of the mon was the doubt they all had because of Donella's insistence that she had killed her captor.

"I doona ken why that crazy woman accused me of kidnapping her," Fraser said after Callum had ignored his complaints.

Callum's hand fisted at his sides and his jaw tightened. "That *woman* is my wife. The one ye petitioned Laird Sutherland to arrange a marriage with. And the only reason I haven't killed ye yet is because we are investigating her charge."

Fraser huffed. "I am The Gunn. I have all the women I need falling at my feet. I doona need to take some scrawny bitch against her will."

Callum's fist flew out before he e'en kenned it. Fraser went flying across the room, landing on his arse with a surprised look on his face.

Callum walked over to him, stepped on his chest and grabbed his leine at the neck, twisting until Fraser's face was red. "I told ye she is my wife. Anymore disrespect out of yer mouth and I *will* take ye apart piece by piece."

He stood and dusted his hands off. "I see it was a mistake coming here, so I will leave ye now. And I suggest ye spend more time at the lists and less at the supper table. Ye can hardly defend yerself." With those words he kicked his brother on the chin, and left the room, slamming the door shut, the continued surprised look on Fraser's face bringing him a smile.

Aye, it had no' been a good idea to try to speak with Fraser.

During a brief meeting after supper, Haydon, Conall,

and Callum spent time speaking of the issues they were facing.

"Based on the information ye gave me earlier, I sent a rider out this afternoon to find the cottage of that woman who delivered yer brother years ago," Haydon said. "Bringing her here to speak with me will give us something to send to the king to have him relieve Fraser of his lairdship and give it to ye."

"And what about Donella's charge against The Gunn?" Callum asked.

Haydon sighed. "'Tis not an easy one. I'm sending men out tomorrow to see if they can find this cottage where Donella said she'd been held. I realize it's been a long time, but mayhap there is something there that might help us."

After that, Callum took another swim in the cold loch since he figured he was facing another night of frustration in his bed. Then after a few mugs of ale, then two glasses of whisky, he was feeling quite nice.

Callum entered their bedchamber quietly. 'Twas silent and dark. His wife lay on the bed, curled up, hugging his pillow. Her nighttime braid had loosened, and beautiful, silky locks fell over her cheek.

Donella had not appeared for supper in the great hall but after he asked Ainslee, he learned that she had taken a tray in her room. Thinking she was still recovering from her day, he let her be and spent the time speaking with Haydon and Conall.

Seeing his beautiful wife settled in their bed all soft and warm, had his cock rising for the occasion. He sighed, kenning that this was probably the worst night to attempt to make love to her.

But he wanted her so much it hurt.

As he sat on the bed, she opened her eyes, and he was lost. "Good evening, husband," she whispered.

He reached out and ran his knuckles down her warm, soft cheek. "Aye. Good evening to ye as well."

She leaned up on one elbow, pushing back the hair that fell on her shoulder. "Callum?"

"Aye, love."

"I want ye to make love to me."

He thought his cock would explode. For a few moments he couldn't speak, making sure he'd heard what she'd said. "Are ye sure, lass? Do ye ken what yer asking?"

Please, good Lord, doona let her change her mind.

"I am sure. I ken how much ye love me, and how much I love ye. I ken it will be so different than what I had before." She reached out and touched his cheek. "'Tis been too long. I want ye, Callum. I want to be yer wife in truth."

He'd ne'er removed his clothes so fast in his life. Within seconds he was in bed with her. "Are ye really sure, lass?

"Aye. I want to replace the bad memories with good ones."

"Ach, lass. I can give so many good memories it will last for the rest of yer life." He stopped for a minute, thinking about what he'd just said. "Ne'er mind, darling, we need a lifetime for me to show ye how much I love ye." Callum leaned down and took Donella in a searing, loving, possessive kiss.

* * *

Donella was ne'er surer of anything in her life. Facing her captor and then spending time with Angus learning how to use a weapon gave her a feeling of strength.

Remembering what Dorathia told her about how growing wet in her woman's parts when Callum kissed her and touched her, she felt secure that when the time came for the actual 'act' she would not feel pain.

"Sweetheart, I can hear ye thinking," Callum said as he moved his mouth down to pay attention to her breasts. "Do ye ken what that means?"

"Nay." Feelings that she'd tried to hide when they'd cuddled and touched before flowed through her. This time she welcomed them and wanted more.

"If yer thinking, then I'm no' doing my job," he mumbled as he continued to kiss and suckle her breasts.

She squirmed and her feet moved back and forth. "Can I touch ye, Callum?"

"Aye, lass. Touch all ye want."

Tentatively, she slid her hand down his chest until she reached his man parts. He moaned as she gripped him. "Ach, 'tis sorry I am. Did I hurt ye?"

"Nay, it feels good. Ye caught me by surprise."

She found once she touched him, it seemed like she'd broken through a barrier. He felt soft and hard, warm and odd. She still thought it was too big to fit inside her, but Dorathia had told her to relax and enjoy what her husband did to get her ready.

Callum was nipping on her nipple with his teeth and the scratching and tugging was building up something in her body she'd ne'er felt before.

"Are ye well, Donella?" he asked as he switched from

one breast to the other while his hand moved down to the area between her legs.

Even though he couldn't see her, she smiled. "Aye, I am verra well."

His thumb had found a piece of flesh that he rubbed in a circle making her breath catch and more moisture gather. He moved his mouth up from her breast to take her mouth in a searing kiss. His movements were surprisingly and touchingly restrained.

The gentle massage with his thumb sent currents of desire through her. She dinna ken what it was she wanted but had a feeling her husband kenned and would do exactly what she needed.

His mouth moved from her mouth to the soft skin under her ear. He kissed the sensitive skin and then sucked on her ear lobe. Who kenned that something like that would feel so good?

As his warm breath flowed over her, his heartbeat throbbed against her ear.

"I think ye like that, lass," he said, braced on his elbows and staring into her eyes.

"I do. I like it verra much."

"Ach, Donella. Yer so beautiful I canna believe yer mine." He brushed the hair off her forehead with his thumbs. She felt her breasts crushed against his strong chest. She rubbed her body back and forth against his.

Callum groaned and his mouth covered hers hungrily. She gripped his hair with her fingers, tugging as he continued his assault.

Her hands wandered from his strong shoulders to his muscular back down to his tight buttocks. His body was so verra different from hers. Where she was soft, he was hard.

His fingers once again moved to the area between her thighs. "Ach, my love, ye are ready for me."

She stiffened slightly when she felt Callum's finger enter her. "Be at ease, sweetheart."

"'Tis all fine, husband." Once again she relaxed her legs, letting them drop open.

"That's my lass," he said, once more taking her mouth in a kiss that demanded surrender.

She was ready to surrender. She loved this mon with her whole heart and wanted to give him what he deserved and what she kenned would be a wonderful experience for her, as well.

Callum shifted his body until he rested completely on hers, snuggly settled between her legs. He continued to kiss her as he placed his man part at the entrance to her body.

She took a verra deep breath, telling herself this was Callum, her husband who loved her verra much. He had prepared her body for this and 'twould be fine.

He cupped her cheeks, his deep green eyes almost black as he stared at her. "I love ye, Donella," he said as he slid into her body.

She tightened for a moment, then when she felt no pain, just a sense of fullness, she relaxed. It felt so good. In fact, so verra good.

"Are ye well, lass?"

"Aye. I feel strange, but fine."

He began to move slowly, and then shifted a bit so he was able to place his thumb once again on the piece of flesh that had seemed to swell since he'd last touched it.

"Ach, Callum, that feels good."

He grunted his answer and moved his body so he could slide in and out, giving her a great deal of pleasure. But what he was doing with his thumb was e'en better.

Once more his mouth covered hers as he moved in a rhythm so that he brought e'en more wonderful feelings to her. She wrapped her legs around his hips and pressed her body against his. "Callum, I feel as though I need something else."

"Aye, lass. Just relax and it will come."

She did as he said and within less than a minute something exploded in her head just as Callum pushed hard against her and pulled her close as he pumped in and out. His groan matched hers as he stiffened, and she felt warm liquid enter her body. They held each other so tight, 'twas almost as if they wanted to meld their bodies together.

Callum collapsed and rolled off her. They were both breathing heavily, and she was covered with sweat. He pulled her close. "I love ye, wife."

"And I love ye, husband," she said.

After a few minutes they grew cold, and Callum reached down and drew the coverlet over them. Turning to his side, he wrapped his arm around Donella's waist and pulled her next to him until their bodies were fitted snugly together.

Had she kenned how wonderful love making would be with the mon she loved, she would have gotten over her fears much sooner.

Almost as if he read her thoughts, he mumbled as she was drifting off the sleep, "'Twas the right time, my love."

* * *

OLD MARTA ARRIVED at the castle two days later. The Gunns were still holed up in one of the bedchambers, but were given the best of meals and drink. Haydon still insisted on this since there hadn't been any proof yet that The Gunn was guilty of either charge and, as a laird, he was due respect.

Callum helped the midwife from the cart that brought her to the castle. She smiled at him and patted his hand as he walked her to the keep.

Haydon met them at the door of the keep and thanked her for coming.

"Aye, my laird, 'tis with a great pleasure that I get to see ye again."

Once they reached his solar and Haydon requested refreshments be brought for the woman, he settled back in his chair and studied her.

"The reason we brought ye here is because we intend to confront Fraser Gunn with what ye told us the other day. He has been here for a few days now. We had intended to present this information to him, but decided it was best to hear it directly from ye. I assume ye doona have an objection to repeating yer story to him?"

"Nay. It always troubled me that Lady Gunn allowed one son to deny the other son his rightful place."

Ainslee shrugged. "It seems to me she might have been reluctant to admit she was carrying a bairn when she married The Gunn."

"Aye," Old Marta said. "From what I understood, she was in love with Fraser's da, but her parents arranged her marriage to strengthen an alliance between the Gunns and the Sinclairs."

"No'hing strange about that," Haydon said. "My marriage was an arranged one."

Ainslee coughed and Haydon turned and smiled at her. Donella had told him that the arranged marriage for the laird had been between Haydon and Ainslee's twin sister, Elsbeth. The twin was a meek woman, prone to fainting and terrified of the laird.

Unbeknownst to Haydon, the lasses switched places before the wedding, eventually making for a perfect match between the laird and his wife who had no problem standing up to the laird. No fainting for Lady Sutherland.

"I think it's time to bring The Gunn down from the bedchamber where he's been for days and let Marta tell her story in front of him," Haydon said. He nodded at one of the warriors lining the walls of the solar.

Callum reached over and took Donella's hand in his, resting them on his thigh.

Within minutes Fraser Gunn and the rest of his men entered the room. He scowled at Callum who noticed that his brother had a bruise on his chin where Callum had kicked him.

"What is this, Sutherland?" He groused the minute he entered the room. "I thought ye invited me here for a meeting about our borders and I've been insulted, held prisoner, attacked by the traitor, and now this looks like some kind of a court."

"Take a seat, Gunn. There is something we need to address."

Fraser glanced over at Donella with a look that had Callum stiffening. He squeezed Donella's hand, but when he glanced over at her, she had raised her chin and stared Fraser right back in the eyes. He looked away.

Score one for ye, lass.

"There is some question about the Gunn lairdship."

Fraser jumped up. Conall immediately withdrew his sword. "What devil is this, Sutherland? I demand ye return our swords and we will be on our way. Ye apparently have nothing of interest to me to discuss. Ye can hold yer court without us. And for certes the king will hear about this."

"Sit down, Gunn," Haydon said. He turned to Old Marta. "Would ye mind telling Fraser Gunn what ye told us?"

Callum noticed that Haydon had not referred to Fraser with the proper title.

Old Marta repeated her story, and it was apparent to Callum as he watched his brother that this was no' a story with which he was unfamiliar.

When the woman was finished, Fraser was on his feet again, and Callum's sword was in his hand once more.

"This is outrageous! I willna stand for this. Again, I demand a return of our weapons." He wagged his finger at Haydon. "I doona ken what game ye are playing, but ye can be sure King Charles will hear about this. And ye are growing close for this nonsense to be declared an act of war!"

"I intend to inform the king of this situation myself," Haydon said. He waved Fraser to a seat again. "Once more I ask ye to sit." He turned to one of the warriors against the wall. "Please escort Marta to one of the bedchambers where she can rest."

He smiled at the woman. "Thank ye for coming. I

would be pleased if ye would join us for supper and then stay the night before your return home."

Once they left the room, Haydon said. "We now have another charge against ye."

Fraser immediately looked over at Donella and Callum was now ready to beat the mon senseless. 'Twas for certes he kenned exactly what was coming and 'twas no surprise for him.

Haydon cleared his throat. "Donella, will ye please tell Fraser what you've told us."

Donella stared directly at Fraser as she told him exactly what he'd done to her. He was ne'er more proud of his wife. Callum stared at the mon the entire time. A tad of surprise, guilt, and anger flashed over his face.

Donella was shaking and taking deep breaths when she finished. Callum studied Fraser.

Instead of the anger he expected, he waved his hand. "'Tis no' true. I have no idea who abducted the lass, but it wasna me and ye canna tell me she remembered it from all those years ago."

Haydon leaned forward, his voice barely above a whisper. "The lass dinna say it was many years ago."

Callum realized Haydon was right. Donella never mentioned when it happened, only what took place. Once that thought sank into his brain, with a strangled cry he jumped up and threw himself at his brother.

They went down with a crash, fists flying.

17

Hysteria reigned in Haydon's solar. Malcolm attempted to pull Callum off Fraser, Sutherland warriors whipped out their swords and backed Gunn's men to the wall.

Haydon drew his sword and placed it to Gunn's throat. "Callum, get off him."

"Nay! He violated my wife. And beat her. I'm going to kill him."

"No yer not!" Haydon roared. "Now back up."

Before obeying his laird, Callum threw one solid punch to Fraser's face, knocking him out.

"Why dinna ye let him kill the bastard?" Conall said, returning his sword to his side.

"Because the mon is Laird of Gunn. If he is to be punished, 'twill be the right of King Charles. Despite our feelings about the mon and what he did to our sister and Callum's wife, we need the king to decide his fate. We also need Charles to decide on the right to the lairdship. These are no' decisions we can make because since the king has been newly restored to the Crown, and he has made it clear he doesna want war between the clans which is exactly what this would turn into."

Conall stared at Fraser, still knocked out, lying on the floor. "What do we do with them?"

"Lock them all in the dungeon. We have witnesses to the charges now, so the Gunns are all prisoners. I will send a missive post haste to the Crown to see what is to be done with them."

"And if we get no response? Aside from the dictate we received from Charles about keeping the peace between the clans, no one has heard from him," Conall said.

"Then we decide, but for now, lock them up."

Callum stalked from the room. Donella stood to go after him but Haydon stopped her with his hand on her shoulder. "Let him go, lass. He needs to work off his anger." Haydon turned to Conall. "As do ye, brother."

Conall nodded and followed Callum out. Haydon walked over to his desk and sat, his elbows braced on the desk, his head in his hands.

Donella approached him. "Doona fash yerself, brother. 'Twill all work out."

"Nay." He looked up at her. "I donna have any faith in Charles answering any missive I send. The mon is only recently restored to his rightful place and I'm sure he has much on his mind besides two clans battling each other."

* * *

A WEEK HAD GONE BY, and there had been no return missive from the king. From what the guards at the dungeon had told them the Gunns were making a lot of noise and demands.

"How much longer are ye going to let those bastards sit in the dungeon? I'm all for hanging The Gunn," Conall said as he joined Haydon and Callum at the dais while they drank mugs of ale awaiting the nooning.

"'Too soon yet to make a decision," Haydon said as he drained his mug. "I doona ken if Charles would accept hanging. He's a tad jittery right now with his recent restoration. We doona want the power of the Crown down on our heads. Things are no' stable throughout Scotland. Hanging a laird, no matter what the charges, could be considered an act of war against the king."

"Aye, but if ye hang Fraser, then I am laird by default. I willna wage war on ye," Callum said.

"Yer no' the king," Haydon answered.

Callum ne'er thought he would say those words about his brother, and e'en him conspiring with their mam to take the lairdship for himself wouldna have him wanting to see the mon hanged.

But what he'd done to Donella was a hanging offense as far as he was concerned. In fact, any sort of death for the mon would be justified. Preferably slow and painful.

He thought of the times when they were younger, and the best of friends. They'd had so much fun together and had gotten into enough trouble to lose their supper a few times.

'Twas a shame his mam's deceit turned Fraser into the mon he was now. Strangely enough, Callum had ne'er wanted the lairdship. He kenned that once Da died and Fraser inherited the lairdship, he would be his second-in-command and the lairdship would only be his if Fraser died before him. But he ne'er desired it.

He was happy with this role as one of his da's second-in-command. He'd expected one day he would marry a lovely lass and have a family. The idea of power and leadership ne'er entered his head.

Kidnapping Donella and doing such horrible things to her was more shocking to him than his other charge. For that he thought Fraser should lose his life. And he would be more than happy to run his sword through the mon.

Donella entered the great hall, apparently having spent the morning with Dorathia. She was verra happy to be helping the healer and learning the craft. If he was, in fact, expected to take over the Gunn Clan, it would be good for her to be able to use her skills there.

That brought him to the thought he hadn't really dwelt too much on. He had sworn his loyalty to Haydon and expected to stay here with his wife and future family for the rest of his life.

Now he was forcing his wife to leave her home. But 'twas what all women did when they married outside their clan. And the Gunn castle was no' far from Dornoch.

They'd made love at least once e'ery night and she was as responsive as any mon would be happy with. She had even begun to be the one who initiated their love making and that charmed him more than anything.

"Dorathia received good news today," Donella said as she joined him on the dais. "Her niece, Helena is on her way back to Dornoch."

"Where was the lass?"

"She had gone to visit her sister who had just given birth to her first bairn. She married a Mackay and Helena had been there for at least a couple of months now, Dorathia said."

"Is she a healer, also?"

"Aye. Dorathia had been training her. She also had been training me, as ye ken, and now if we move to Gunn Castle, she will lose me, so 'tis good Helena should be here soon."

He covered her hand with his as it rested on the table. "How do ye feel about that, wife? As ye say, if I am granted the lairdship, we will need to move."

She shrugged. "As long as ye are with me, husband, I doona care where I live. I will for sure miss my family, but a woman's place is with her husband."

"Thank ye, love. I dinna think ye would have a problem with it, but I wanted to make sure since we're facing so many issues right now."

"No word from the king, then?" she asked.

"Nay."

He smiled at her, thinking about how Donella bravely confronted Fraser. She had filled him with pride.

The serving lasses came from the kitchen with platters of roasted vegetables, cheese, bread, and bowls of stewed apples.

"When I left Gunn Castle several months ago, the healer there, Ceit Gunn, was getting on in years." Callum placed food from the platters into their bread trencher. "She could certainly use yer help."

Conversation ceased as they all ate their meal. Callum spent the time going over what his new duties would be once he was named laird. Of course, if and when the king arrived, or ordered them to travel to court, it would be up to him whether he believed the old woman's story or no'.

TO CHARM A HIGHLANDER

Then again, if he believed Donella's story, no' only would Fraser lose the lairdship, he could verra well be executed for his crime. After all, Donella was Lady Donella of Sutherland, sister to the Laird of Sutherland, no' some doxy from an ale house. A crime committed against her was a verra serious matter.

* * *

DONELLA SPENT the rest of the day working with Dorathia. Now that it appeared she would be doing her healing at Gunn Castle, she was anxious to learn as much as she could.

She climbed off the stool she had been using to crush herbs and make potions for Dorathia to store until needed. Then they spent time washing linen strips of cloth, then laying them out in the back of the cottage to dry in the scant sun.

After giving herself a good-feeling stretch, she decided to find Angus and practice her knife-throwing and self-protection moves he'd taught her. She turned to Dorathia who was just adding jars of healing cream up on the shelf where she stored her medicants. "I think I will take a walk over to the keep. 'Tis growing close to supper and I want to wash up before I join Callum."

"Ye won't be walking anywhere, lass."

Donella turned at the voice and immediately Fraser stepped into the room and grabbed her before she could process what was going on. He wrapped his arm around her waist and pulled her against his body, putting a knife to her throat.

"What are ye doing? Ye are supposed to be in the

dungeon." She spoke softly, not wanting the blade to slit her throat.

"Ye have to be careful who ye think ye can trust. All it takes is a few sweet words to the lass bringing my food." He looked over at Dorathia who watched the two of them with fear in her eyes.

"Doona hurt her," she said, wringing her hands.

"Nay, she is my way out of this blasted place. Now, ye are going to find Haydon Sutherland and bring him here. If ye take too long, I just might give the lass a few stabs."

Dorathia raced from the cottage.

"Ye will ne'er get away with this, ye ken," Donella said. She used the new strength she'd found within herself.

Fraser pushed the knife closer to her neck. She backed her head up so it was actually resting on Fraser's chest. She felt a small nick and blood running down her neck.

"'Tis better to keep yer mouth shut, lass. Every time ye speak I will give ye another scratch with my knife." He leaned in next to her ear. "I remember ye, lass. I owe you for stabbing me and leaving me to die in that cottage." He pulled her closer and moved the knife flat against her throat. "Ye weren't worth my time, ye ken. Ye were too scared, and nothing I hate more than a weeping virgin."

"Ye should have let me go, then."

"'Twas too much fun to watch the sister of the important Laird Sutherland at my mercy." He leaned in even farther. "I had great plans for ye, lass."

She struggled to keep her last meal down at the smell of the mon.

Please God, help me out of this without anyone being killed.

Despite feeling as though so much time had passed since Dorathia had left, 'twas no more than five minutes when Haydon, Conall, and Callum crowded through the front door, their swords drawn.

"Ah, the Sutherland men. And my traitor brother who pledged his loyalty to the laird and even married wearing Sutherland plaid."

Callum opened his mouth to respond, but Haydon placed his hand on his shoulder and pressed. "Do no' provoke him."

"I will kill him," Callum muttered.

"Nay, traitor, ye won't kill me because if any of ye move one more step forward, ye will watch as I slit yer wife's throat."

"Loosen yer hold on the lass, and then we can talk," Haydon said.

Fraser complied and Callum drew a deep breath.

"What do ye want to let my sister go?" Haydon said.

"'Tis glad I am that ye asked. I want my horse. And my weapons."

"Ye can have them. Just let Donella go."

"Nay. Now ye see, I have a little problem that ye are going to help me with. I am taking the lass here to my castle where she will remain until I receive word from the king that I am the true Laird of Gunn and any charges against me for what happened to the lass has been dismissed."

"Ye do understand ye are declaring war on the Sutherlands?"

"Aye, ye are correct. Mayhap I will keep the lass then for at least a year to make certes ye doona attack me."

"Ye can't keep her for a year. I willna allow it!" Callum shouted.

Fraser dragged her backward until he hit the wall. "Ye

are taking a chance, traitor. Ye may think the three of ye against me will end with my death. That might be true, but I'll take the lass with me to hell if even one of ye makes a move toward me."

Donella could see the fear and anger in Callum's eyes and stance. They were in a standoff.

"Ye will get me my horse and weapons, Sutherland, and call off yer guards. Yer sister's life is at stake here." Fraser studied the three men and tightened his grip on her body.

Haydon moved away from the door. "Take the lass outside and we'll get yer horse and yer weapons for ye."

Fraser shook his head. "Nay. I'll stay right here until ye tell me the horse is ready and my weapons are at my side. And then I'll only move if the keep is cleared and ye and yer men are nowhere in sight."

Donella kenned she would not go with Fraser no matter what. She would rather he slit her throat than go through what she'd gone through before with the mon.

"Get his horse," Haydon growled at one of the guards.

"And get my men up here," Fraser added. "They're still stuck in the dungeon. And I'll want their horses and weapons returned, too."

Donella's heart pounded and her stomach cramped with fear. E'en with her husband two brothers in the same room with her, they couldna save her. One move from any of them and Fraser was crazy enough to kill her.

"When my men arrive, ye will all leave the keep and I doona want to see any of ye, or yer sister—and *wife*—" he glanced at his brother with a smirk, "will die."

He stared at Callum and after a few seconds said, "How does it feel keening I had yer wife before ye did?"

Haydon wrapped his arm around Callum's chest to keep him from running toward his brother.

"Remain still," Haydon barked. "He is crazy enough to slice her throat."

"Verra smart, laird," Fraser said. He waited about a tense minute before bellowing, "Where are my men? And where are the horses?" His hold on her remained the same, but he shifted when he shouted, and loosened the hand that held the knife to her throat.

Donella used that moment of distraction to apply a movement Angus had taught her. Either this would work, or she would die looking at her beloved husband across the room.

With swiftness even she dinna ken she possessed, but assumed was from desperation, she linked her fingers, moved her arms straight out and with all her strength, she slammed her elbow into Fraser's middle.

The mon was a warrior, so she dinna plan on hurting him, but she did accomplish what she'd intended. The shock of her movement caused Fraser to drop the knife. Before anyone else could react, she bent and grabbed the knife and plunged it into his chest with the force of all the stored up anger she felt. He fell to the ground like a wounded boar.

Donella turned and raced into Callum's arms. Haydon and Conall strode up to Fraser. Haydon bent down on one knee and placed his fingers on the mon's neck. "Ye did it this time, lass. The knife went straight into his heart. He's dead."

Confusion reigned as the Gunn prisoners were brought up to the solar from the dungeon. Callum still couldna believe his wee wife had saved herself from the brute.

He held her close as she shook and cried. The questions he had could wait until she calmed down.

Haydon walked to where the Gunn warriors were, the shocked look on their faces as they stared at Fraser was almost amusing. "Callum is yer laird now. Either kneel and swear yer loyalty to him, or ye will spend the rest of yer days in the dungeon."

Without hesitation the men knelt before him and pledged their allegiance. Callum nodded as each mon spoke. He kenned the men since he'd lived at the castle his whole life before Fraser threw him out.

He had no idea how much loyalty would be offered to him by the rest of the Gunn clan, but that wasna something he concerned himself with now.

"My love, I think it would be a good idea to leave the room." Even though Donella had killed the mon, 'twas no' wise to have her standing there staring at his dead body.

"Aye, husband. What I would like is a small cup of whisky, and then a walk in the gardens. The scent of the herbs and flowers will calm me."

Thinking it a strange request but wanting to get her as far away as he could, they left.

Since it was nearing the supper hour and no one except those in Dorathia's cottage had kenned what had happened, the great room was filling up, becoming noisy, lively, and…normal.

After downing a cup of whisky, Callum took Donella's hand and led her to the back of the keep. Almost as a liberation, the sun broke through the clouds as they stepped out of the keep and entered the garden.

They dinna speak for a while, just strolled and enjoyed the scent and sight of herbs and flowers.

They sat on a stone bench that separated the herb garden from the vegetable garden. "Do ye feel as though ye can speak now, sweetheart?"

Donella sighed deeply and stared at the beautiful gardens so well taken care of. "Aye. I am at ease now."

Callum grinned. "I imagine the whisky had something to do with it." He turned to her. "How the devil did ye learn what ye did back there that saved ye when three of the best warriors in the Highlands were stuck there unable to do a damned thing?"

She smiled and he kenned right then that what had happened to her would not cause her to retreat once again. "I've been practicing knife throwing with Angus, the stablemaster. It started as a way to make me feel more powerful, and in control of myself. While training me, he added in various moves I could do to protect myself, including how to escape a mon's hold." She shook her head. "Ne'er did I expect to have to use it so soon."

Callum shook his head. "Ye are an amazing woman, wife." He leaned over and kissed her thoroughly, with promises of more to come.

EPILOGUE

Callum held Donella's hair back as she retched into the chamber pot in their bedchamber. 'Twas almost two weeks now that she'd been doing the same thing each morning.

They'd been at Gunn Castle for a month and things had settled down nicely once they'd arrived from Dornoch. It had appeared that Fraser had no' made many friends as laird and the servants greeted him with open affection, and tales of Fraser's beating of servants and chasing the serving lasses all o'er the castle.

"'Twas no' a safe place for the women while he was laird," Maddie, the cook told Callum. "I ne'er understood how being brothers, the two of ye were so different."

Callum and Donella had looked at each other, but dinna say anything. With the mon dead, there was no reason to besmirch his mam's reputation with the clan.

"I think I can concede that I am with child, Callum," Donella said as he handed her a cup of water to rinse out her mouth.

"Aye, so it seems, lass. I notice ye haven't had yer woman's time since we began to share a bed."

Donella blushed and shoved the mug at him. "Ye shouldn't speak of those things, husband."

Callum threw back his head and laughed. "Donella, love, we've done more than share a bed. After some of the things we've done—"

"—Stop!" She walked over to the bed and reached for her chemise. "'This no' proper."

He walked up behind her and wrapped his arms around her waist. He patted her flat stomach with his hand. "Ye will be quite rounded soon." He turned her so she faced him and lifted her chin with his knuckle.

"When I married ye, I thought all I had to offer was my sword and honor. Now it seems ye will be mam to the next Laird of Gunn."

She smirked at him. "I'm growing cold, husband."

He patted her on her naked backside and released her. She drew her chemise and dress over her head and shimmied until they fell into place.

"Do ye remember I told ye Haydon and Ainslee are coming for a visit?" Donella said as she braided her hair.

"Nay. I've been so busy with getting the warriors in better shape that I haven't been paying much attention to anything else. When are they expected?"

"On the morrow. I think my brother is interested in seeing that his little sister is happy and well settled."

Callum huffed. "If ye were any happier we'd ne'er get anything done."

She stopped tying the bodice of her dress. "What does that mean?"

He pulled her toward him and finished tying the laces. "I ken I make ye happy in our bed."

"Sheesh! Do ye think about anything else, husband?"

He nuzzled her neck. "Nay."

THE NEXT DAY, Donella reached for wee Finlay and took the lad from Ainslee's arms as they entered the keep. "I swear, sister, he is bigger than when we left just a month ago."

Ainslee handed the bairn over. "With the way he eats I expect him to be bigger than his da before he's seen fifteen summers."

Haydon and Ainslee had just arrived from Dornoch Castle for their visit. After kisses and hugs, and with a couple of hours before supper, the two women walked up to Donella's solar with all four children and settled on the comfortable settees and chairs.

The men had disappeared, most likely to Callum's solar for a cup of whisky or two.

The little ones played on the floor with the toys Ainslee produced from the satchel she carried.

"How are ye finding life at Gunn Castle?" Ainslee asked as she tugged the hem of her dress from Finlay's mouth. "This lad will chew on anything." She reached into her satchel and removed a sock wrapped around some sort of object and handed it to the little one.

"What is that?" Donella asked.

"'Tis a teething sock. I learned from Jonet who had several bairns before I did on how to make one."

"Well, ye will have to tell me how to make one soon," Donella said with a smile on her lips.

Ainslee offered her a bright smile. "Are ye with child, then lass?"

"Aye. It appears so. I've been sick e'ery morn for about two weeks, I haven't had my woman's time in a while and I canna abide food until close to the nooning. Then I eat everything in sight."

Ainslee nodded. "It appears ye are right. That's all the signs. Do ye have a midwife here?"

"Aye. Me." She laughed. "Ceit Gunn has been the healer for many years, but she has grown old and I've been helping her with the sick and also the expecting mothers." She shook her head. "I have no idea what I'm to do when my time comes."

"When the time comes, I will send Helena over to help ye," Ainslee said.

A young serving lass came into the solar with a tray of ale for the ladies and milk for the little ones.

Once they were all settled again, Donella asked, "So Helena has returned to Dornoch from Mackay land?"

"Aye. She arrived about two weeks after ye left."

"How is she faring?"

Ainslee stopped and stared at the wall for a minute. "I doona ken what to say. She is different somehow. No' as cheerful as she's always been."

Callum and Haydon entered the solar. Haydon threw Alasdair up in the air and the lad immediately emptied the contents of his stomach on his da's head.

"I told ye before no' to do that, husband." Ainslee shook her head and pulled a cloth out of her satchel. "The lad seems to have a delicate stomach."

"Nay," Haydon said. "No son of mine will have a delicate anything."

"Doona be ridiculous," Ainslee said. "He canna help it if he has one."

In order to stop the bickering she could see coming, Donella asked, "Did ye tell my brother about the bairn?"

Callum ran his fingers through his hair. "Nay. I forgot."

Donella sucked in a breath. "Ye forgot!"

"'Tis sorry, I am, lass." He turned to Haydon. "Ye will be an uncle again, brother. Mayhap in about seven months."

Haydon slapped Callum on the back. "Quick work, lad. I hope ye have many bairns to keep the castle noisy."

Ainslee picked up Alasdair, placed him on her lap and took a wooden toy horse out of his mouth. "Aye, many bairns. Just no' all in a row like we did."

"I'm thinking, wife, that 'tis time for another bairn."

"Well, think that do ye, husband? Ye can carry the next one. Ye can be the one with swollen feet, and a sore back and a sour stomach."

Haydon sat next to his wife. "Now, *mo chridhe*, ye ken I canna do that." He placed his hand on his chest. "If I could save ye the suffering, I would."

Ainslee smirked. "Aye, I'm sure ye would. And complain the entire time."

"I am a warrior, woman, I doona complain."

"Aye, ye do. Every time ye get the ague, I have to listen to yer suffering."

"I doona suffer."

Callum reached for Donella's hand. They walked from the room, grinning. "I think we can find something to do to keep ourselves occupied before supper instead of listening to them argue."

"Ye ken they only argue because they love each other," Donella said.

One of the bairns began to wail as Callum and Donella reached their bedchamber door and slipped inside.

Many bairns, indeed.

Did you like this story? Please consider leaving a review on either Goodreads or the place where you bought it. Long or short, your review will help other readers discover new authors and make purchasing decisions!

I hope you had fun reading Donella and Callum's love story. Want more Highlander romance? *Never Fall for a Highlander* is the first book in a new spin-off series, The Mackays of Varrich Castle. Watch for the release of midwife Helena Sutherland's story in Spring 2024.

ABOUT THE AUTHOR

Receive a free book and stay up to date with new releases and sales!
http://calliehutton.com/newsletter/

USA Today bestselling author, Callie Hutton, has penned more than 55 historical romance and cozy mystery books. She lives in Oklahoma with her very close and lively family, which includes her twin grandsons, affectionately known as "The Twinadoes."

Callie loves to hear from readers. Contact her directly at calliehutton11@gmail.com or find her online at www.calliehutton.com.

Connect with her on Facebook, Twitter, and Goodreads.

Follow her on BookBub to receive notice of new releases, preorders, and special promotions.

Praise for books by Callie Hutton

A Study in Murder

"This book is a delight!...*A Study in Murder* has clear echoes of Jane Austen, Agatha Christie, and of course, Sherlock Holmes. You will love this book." —William Bernhardt, author of *The Last Chance Lawyer*

"A one-of-a-kind new series that's packed with surprises." —Mary Ellen Hughes, National bestselling author of *A Curio Killing*.

"[A] lively and entertaining mystery...I predict a long run for this smart series." —Victoria Abbott, award-winning author of The Book Collector Mysteries

"With a breezy style and alluring, low-keyed humor, Hutton crafts a charming mystery with a delightful, irrepressible sleuth." —Madeline Hunter, *New York Times* bestselling author of *Never Deny a Duke*

The Elusive Wife

"I loved this book and you will too. Jason is a hottie & Oliva is the kind of woman we'd all want as a friend. Read it!" —Cocktails and Books

"In my experience I've had a few hits but more misses

with historical romance so I was really pleasantly surprised to be hooked from the start by obviously good writing." —Book Chick City

"The historic elements and sensory details of each scene make the story come to life, and certainly helps immerse the reader in the world that Olivia and Jason share." —The Romance Reviews

"You will not want to miss *The Elusive Wife*." —My Book Addiction

"…it was a well written plot and the characters were likeable." —Night Owl Reviews

A Run for Love

"An exciting, heart-warming Western love story!" —*New York Times* bestselling author Georgina Gentry

"I loved this book!!! I read the BEST historical romance last night…It's called *A Run For Love*." —*New York Times* bestselling author Sharon Sala

"This is my first Callie Hutton story, but it certainly won't be my last." —The Romance Reviews

An Angel in the Mail

"…a warm fuzzy sensuous read. I didn't put it down until I was done." —Sizzling Hot Reviews

Visit www.calliehutton.com for more information.

Printed in Great Britain
by Amazon